THE STRANGE CASE OF
DR. JEKYLL AND MR. HYDE

AND

TRAVELS WITH A DONKEY

DR. JEKYLL
AND
MR. HYDE

by Robert Louis Stevenson

BOOKS, INC., PUBLISHERS • NEW YORK

EDITORIAL NOTE

THE plot of THE STRANGE CASE OF DR. JEKYLL AND MR. HYDE, one of Stevenson's greatest successes, presented itself to him in his sleep. The dream was so startling and so real that his exclamations of horror and his moaning disturbed his wife, who immediately awoke him. This brought down upon her head wrathful remonstrances, as the dream had not been brought to a conclusion. The next morning while the horror of the thing was fresh in his memory and every incident standing out with startling vividness, he wrote the story, the first rough draft being completed in less than three days. Becoming convinced that he had not treated the story in the proper form from a psychological point of view, the first draft was burned and the second written, again in three days.

The book was printed in the latter part of the year 1885 with the intention of offering it for sale during the holiday season. It was withheld, however, until January, 1886, and did not attract much attention until a review appeared in the *Times*, under date of January 25th, 1886, calling attention to the story. From then on the book had a tremendous sale and it is estimated that in its various forms in England and America it has reached a sale of over two million copies.

CONTENTS

Dr. Jekyll and Mr. Hyde

Travels With a Donkey

THE STRANGE CASE OF
DR. JEKYLL AND MR. HYDE

THE STRANGE CASE OF
DR. JEKYLL AND MR. HYDE

STORY OF THE DOOR

MR. UTTERSON, the lawyer, was a man of a rugged countenance, that was never lighted by a smile; cold, scanty and embarrassed in discourse; backward in sentiment; lean, long, dusty, dreary, and yet somehow lovable. At friendly meetings, and when the wine was to his taste, something eminently human beaconed from his eye; something indeed which never found its way into his talk, but which spoke not only in these silent symbols of the after-dinner face, but more often and loudly in the acts of his life. He was austere with himself; drank gin when he was alone, to mortify a taste for vintages; and though he enjoyed the theater, had not crossed the doors of one for twenty years. But he had an approved tolerance for others; sometimes wondering, almost with envy, at the high pressure of spirits involved in their misdeeds; and in any extremity inclined to help rather than to reprove. "I incline to Cain's heresy," he used to say, quaintly; "I let my brother go to the devil in his own way." In this character it was frequently his fortune to be the last reputable acquaintance and the last good influence in the lives of down-going men. And to such as these, so long as they came about his chambers, he never marked a shade of change in his demeanor.

No doubt the feat was easy to Mr. Utterson; for he was undemonstrative at the best, and even his friendships seemed to be founded in a similar catholicity of good-nature. It is the mark of a modest man to accept his friendly circle ready-made from the hands of opportunity; and that was the lawyer's way. His friends were those of his own blood, or those whom he had known the longest; his affections, like ivy, were the growth of time, they implied no aptness in the object. Hence, no doubt, the bond that united him to Mr. Richard Enfield, his distant kinsman, the well-known man about town. It was a nut to crack for many, what these two could see in each other, or what subject they could find in common. It was reported by those who encountered them in their Sunday walks, that they said nothing, looked singularly dull, and would hail with obvious relief the appearance of a friend. For all that, the two men put the greatest store by these excursions, counted them the chief jewel of each week, and not only set aside occasions of pleasure, but even resisted the calls of business, that they might enjoy them uninterrupted.

It chanced on one of these rambles that their way led them down a by-street in a busy quarter of London. The street was small and what is called quiet, but it drove a thriving trade on the week day. The inhabitants were all doing well, it seemed, and all emulously hoping to do better still, and laying out the surplus of their gains in coquetry; so that the shop fronts stood along that thoroughfare with an air of invitation, like rows of smiling saleswomen. Even on Sunday, when it veiled its more florid charms and lay comparatively empty of passage, the street shone out in contrast to its dingy neighborhood, like a fire in a forest; and with its freshly painted shutters, well-polished brasses, and general cleanliness and gayety of note, instantly caught and pleased the eye of the passenger.

Two doors from one corner, on the left hand going east, the line was broken by the entry of a court; and just at that point a certain sinister block of building thrust forward its gable on the street. It was two stories high; showed no window, nothing but a door on the lower story and a blind forehead of discolored wall on the upper; and bore in every feature the marks of prolonged and sordid negligence. The door, which was equipped with neither bell nor knocker, was blistered and distained. Tramps slouched into the recess and struck matches on the panels, children kept shop upon the steps; the schoolboy had tried his knife on the moldings; and for close on a generation, no one had appeared to drive away these random visitors or to repair their ravages.

Mr. Enfield and the lawyer were on the other side of the by-street; but when they came abreast of the entry, the former lifted up his cane and pointed.

"Did you ever remark that door?" he asked; and when his companion had replied in the affirmative, "It is connected in my mind," added he, "with a very odd story."

"Indeed?" said Mr. Utterson, with a slight change of voice, "and what was that?"

"Well, it was this way," returned Mr. Enfield; "I was coming home from some place at the end of the world, about three o'clock of a black winter morning, and my way lay through a part of the town where there was literally nothing to be seen but lamps. Street after street, and all the folks asleep—street after street, all lighted up as if for a procession and all as empty as a church—till at last I got into that state of mind when a man listens and listens and begins to long for the sight of a policeman. All at once I saw two figures; one a little man who was stumping along eastward at a good walk, and the other a girl of maybe eight or ten who was running as hard as she was able down a cross street. Well, sir, the two ran into one another naturally enough at the corner; and then came the horrible part of the thing; for the man trampled calmly over the child's body and left her screaming on the ground. It sounds nothing to hear, but it was hellish to see. It wasn't like a man; it was like some damned Juggernaut.

"I gave a view halloa, took to my heels, collared my gentleman, and brought him back to where there was already quite a group about the screaming child. He was perfectly cool and made no resistance, but gave me one look, so ugly that it brought out the sweat on me like running. The people who had turned out were the girl's own family; and pretty soon, the doctor, for whom she had been sent, put in his appearance. Well, the child was not much the worse, more frightened, according to the Sawbones; and there, you might have supposed, would be an end to it. But there was one curious circumstance. I had taken a loathing to my gentleman at first sight. So had the child's family, which was only natural. But the doctor's case was what struck me. He was the usual cut-and-dry apothecary, of no particular age and color, with a strong Edinburgh accent, and about as emotional as a bagpipe. Well, sir, he was like the rest of us; every time he looked at my prisoner, I saw that Sawbones turn sick and white with the desire to kill him. I knew what was in his mind, just as he knew what was in mine; and killing

being out of the question, we did the next best. We told
the man we could and would make such a scandal out of
this, as should make his name stink from one end of London to the other. If he had any friends or any credit, we
undertook that he should lose them. And all the time, as
we were pitching it in red hot, we were keeping the women off him as best we could, for they were as wild as
harpies.

"I never saw a circle of such hateful faces, and there
was the man in the middle, with a kind of black, sneering
coolness—frightened, too, I could see that—but carrying
it off, sir, really like Satan. 'If you choose to make capital
out of this accident,' said he, 'I am naturally helpless. No
gentleman but wishes to avoid a scene,' says he. 'Name
your figure.' Well, we screwed him up to a hundred
pounds for the child's family; he would have clearly liked
to stick out; but there was something about the lot of us
that meant mischief, and at last he struck. The next thing
was to get the money; and where do you think he carried
us but to that place with the door?—whipped out a key,
went in, and presently came back with the matter of ten
pounds in gold and a check for the balance on Coutts',
drawn payable to bearer and signed with a name that I
can't mention, though it's one of the points of my story,
but it was a name at least very well known and often
printed. The figure was stiff; but the signature was good
for more than that, if it was only genuine. I took the liberty of pointing out to my gentleman that the whole business looked apocryphal, and that a man does not, in real
life, walk into a cellar door at four in the morning and
come out of it with another man's check for close upon a
hundred pounds. But he was quite easy and sneering. 'Set

your mind at rest,' says he, 'I will stay with you till the banks open and cash the check myself.' So we all set off, the doctor, and the child's father, and our friend and myself, and passed the rest of the night in my chambers; and next day, when we had breakfasted, went in a body to the bank. I gave in the check myself, and said I had every reason to believe it was a forgery. Not a bit of it. The check was genuine."

"Tut-tut," said Mr. Utterson.

"I see you feel as I do," said Mr. Enfield. "Yes, it's a bad story. For my man was a fellow that nobody could have to do with, a really damnable man; and the person that drew the check is the very pink of the proprieties, celebrated, too, and (what makes it worse) one of your fellows who do what they call good. Blackmail, I suppose; an honest man paying through the nose for some of the capers of his youth. Black Mail House is what I call that place with the door, in consequence. Though even that, you know, is far from explaining all," he added, and with the words fell into a vein of musing.

From this he was recalled by Mr. Utterson asking rather suddenly: "And you don't know if the drawer of the check lives there?"

"A likely place, isn't it?" returned Mr. Enfield. "But I happen to have noticed his address; he lives in some square or other."

"And you never asked about the—place with the door?" said Mr. Utterson.

"No, sir; I had a delicacy," was the reply. "I feel very strongly about putting questions; it partakes too much of the style of the day of judgment. You start a question, and it's like starting a stone. You sit quietly on the top of a hill; and away the stone goes, starting others; and presently some bland old bird (the last you would have thought of) is knocked on the head in his own back garden, and the family have to change their name. No, sir, I make it a rule of mine: the more it looks like Queer Street, the less I ask."

"A very good rule, too," said the lawyer.

"But I have studied the place for myself," continued Mr. Enfield. "It seems scarcely a house. There is no other door, and nobody goes in or out of that one but, once in a great while, the gentleman of my adventure. There are three windows looking on the court on the first floor; none below; the windows are always shut, but they're clean. And then there is a chimney which is generally smoking; so somebody must live there. And yet it's not so sure; for the buildings are so packed together about that court, that it's hard to say where one ends and another begins."

The pair walked on again for awhile in silence; and then, "Enfield," said Mr. Utterson, "that's a good rule of yours."

"Yes, I think it is," returned Enfield.

"But for all that," continued the lawyer, "there's one point I want to ask. I want to ask the name of that man who walked over the child."

"Well," said Mr. Enfield, "I can't see what harm it would do. It was a man of the name of Hyde."

"H'm," said Mr. Utterson. "What sort of a man is he to see?"

"He is not easy to describe. There is something wrong with his appearance; something displeasing, something downright detestable. I never saw a man so disliked, and

yet I scarcely know why. He must be deformed somewhere; he gives a strong feeling of deformity, although I
couldn't specify the point. He's an extraordinary looking man, and yet I really can name nothing out of the
way. No, sir; I can make no hand of it; I can't describe
him. And it's not want of memory; for I declare I can see
him this moment."

Mr. Utterson again walked some way in silence and ob-
viously under a weight of consideration. "You are sure
he used a key?" he inquired at last.

"My dear sir——" began Enfield, surprised out of himself.

"Yes, I know," said Utterson; "I know it must seem
strange. The fact is, if I do not ask you the name of the
other party, it is because I know it already. You see, Richard, your tale has gone home. If you have been inexact in
any point, you had better correct it."

"I think you might have warned me," returned the
other with a touch of sullenness. "But I have been pedan-
tically exact, as you call it. The fellow had a key; and
what's more, he has it still. I saw him use it, not a week
ago."

Mr. Utterson sighed deeply, but said never a word; and
the young man presently resumed. "Here is another lesson to say nothing," said he. "I am ashamed of my long
tongue. Let us make a bargain never to refer to this
again."

"With all my heart," said the lawyer. "I shake hands
on that, Richard."

SEARCH FOR MR. HYDE

THAT evening Mr. Utterson came home to his bachelor house in somber spirits and sat down to dinner without relish. It was his custom of a Sunday, when this meal was over, to sit close by the fire, a volume of some dry divinity on his reading-desk, until the clock of the neighboring church rang out the hour of twelve, when he would go soberly and gratefully to bed. On this night, however, as soon as the cloth was taken away, he took up a candle and went into his business-room. There he opened his safe, took from the most private part of it a document indorsed on the envelope as Dr. Jekyll's Will, and sat down with a clouded brow to study its contents. The will was holograph, for Mr. Utterson, though he took charge of it now that it was made, had refused to lend the least assistance in the making of it; it provided not only that, in case of the decease of Henry Jekyll, M. D., D. C. L., LL. D., F. R. S., etc., all his possessions were to pass into the hands of his "friend and benefactor, Edward Hyde," but that in case of Dr. Jekyll's "disappearance or unexplained absence for any period exceeding three calendar months," the said Edward Hyde should step into the said Henry Jekyll's shoes without further delay and free from any burden or obligation, beyond the payment of a few small sums to the members of the doctor's household.

This document had long been the lawyer's eyesore. It offended him both as a lawyer and as a lover of the sane and customary sides of life, to whom the fanciful was the immodest. And hitherto it was his ignorance of Mr. Hyde that had swelled his indignation; now, by a sudden turn, it was his knowledge. It was already bad enough when the name was but a name of which he could learn no more. It was worse when it began to be clothed upon with detestable attributes; and out of the shifting, insubstantial mists that had so long baffled his eye, there leaped up the sudden, definite presentment of a fiend.

"I thought it was madness," he said, as he replaced the obnoxious paper in the safe, "and now I begin to fear it is disgrace."

With that he blew out his candle, put on a great-coat and set forth in the direction of Cavendish Square, that citadel of medicine, where his friend, the great Dr. Lanyon, had his house, and received his crowding patients. "If any one knows, it will be Lanyon," he had thought.

The solemn butler knew and welcomed him; he was subjected to no stage of delay, but ushered direct from the door to the dining-room where Dr. Lanyon sat alone over his wine. This was a hearty, healthy, dapper, red-faced gentleman, with a shock of hair prematurely white, and a boisterous and decided manner. At sight of Mr. Utterson, he sprang up from his chair and welcomed him with both hands. The geniality, as was the way of the man, was somewhat theatrical to the eye; but it reposed on genuine feeling. For these two were old friends, old mates both at school and college, both thorough respecters of themselves and of each other, and, what does not always follow, men who thoroughly enjoyed each other's company.

After a little rambling talk the lawyer led up to the subject which so disagreeably preoccupied his mind.

"I suppose, Lanyon," said he, "you and I must be the
two oldest friends that Henry Jekyll has?"

"I wish the friends were younger," chuckled Dr. Lanyon. "But I suppose we are. And what of that? I see little
of him now."

"Indeed?" said Utterson. "I thought you had a bond of
common interest."

"We had," was the reply. "But it is more than ten
years since Henry Jekyll became too fanciful for me. He
began to go wrong, wrong in mind; and though of course
I continue to take an interest in him for old sake's sake,
as they say, I see and I have seen devilish little of the man.
Such unscientific balderdash," added the doctor, flushing
suddenly purple, "would have estranged Damon and
Pythias."

This little spirit of temper was somewhat of a relief to
Mr. Utterson. "They have only differed on some point
of science," he thought; and being a man of no scientific
passions (except in the matter of conveyancing), he even
added, "It is nothing worse than that!" He gave his friend
a few seconds to recover his composure, and then approached the question he had come to put. "Did you ever
come across a *protegé* of his—one Hyde?" he asked.

"Hyde?" repeated Lanyon. "No. Never heard of him.
Since my time."

That was the amount of information that the lawyer
carried back with him to the great, dark bed on which he
tossed to and fro, until the small hours of the morning began to grow large. It was a night of little ease to his toil-

ing mind, toiling in mere darkness, and besieged by questions.

Six o'clock struck on the bells of the church that was so conveniently near to Mr. Utterson's dwelling, and still he was digging at the problem. Hitherto it had touched him on the intellectual side alone; but now his imagination also was engaged or rather enslaved; and as he lay and tossed in the gross darkness of the night and the curtained room, Mr. Enfield's tale went by before his mind in a scroll of lighted pictures. He would be aware of the great field of lamps of a nocturnal city; then of the figure of a man walking swiftly; then of a child running from the doctor's; and then these met, and that human Juggernaut trod the child down and passed on regardless of her screams. Or else he would see a room in a rich house, where his friend lay asleep, dreaming and smiling at his dreams; and then the door of that room would be opened, the curtains of the bed plucked apart, the sleeper recalled, and lo! there would stand by his side a figure to whom power was given, and, even at that dead hour, he must rise and do its bidding. The figure in these two phases haunted the lawyer all night; and if at any time he dozed over it was but to see it glide more stealthily through sleeping houses, or move the more swiftly and still the more swiftly, even to dizziness, through wider labyrinths of lamp-lighted city, and at every street corner crush a child and leave her screaming.

And still the figure had no face by which he might know it; even in his dreams, it had no face, or one that baffled him and melted before his eyes; and thus it was that there sprung up and grew apace in the lawyer's mind

a singularly strong, almost an inordinate, curiosity to behold the features of the real Mr. Hyde. If he could once
set eyes on him, he thought the mystery would lighten
and perhaps roll altogether away, as was the habit of
mysterious things when well examined. He might see a
reason for his friend's strange preference or bondage (call
it which you please), and even for the startling clause of
the will. At least it would be a face worth seeing: the
face of a man who was without bowels of mercy; a face
which had but to show itself to raise up, in the mind of
the unimpressionable Enfield, a spirit of enduring hatred.

From that time forward Mr. Utterson began to haunt
the door in the by-street of shops. In the morning before
office hours, at noon, when business was plenty and time
scarce, at night under the face of the fogged city moon, by
all lights and at all hours of solitude or concourse, the
lawyer was to be found on his chosen post.

"If he be Mr. Hyde," he had thought, "I shall be Mr.
Seek."

And at last his patience was rewarded. It was a fine, dry
night; frost in the air; the streets as clean as a ballroom
floor; the lamps, unshaken by any wind, drawing a regular
pattern of light and shadow. By ten o'clock, when the
shops were closed, the by-street was very solitary and, in
spite of the low growl of London from all around, very
silent. Small sounds carried far; domestic sounds out of
the houses were clearly audible on either side of the roadway; and the rumor of the approach of any passenger preceded him by a long time. Mr. Utterson had been some
minutes at his post, when he was aware of an odd, light
footstep drawing near. In the course of his nightly patrols
he had long grown accustomed to the quaint effect with

which the footfalls of a single person, while he is still a great way off, suddenly spring out distinct from the vast hum and clatter of the city. Yet his attention had never before been so sharply and decisively arrested; and it was with a strong, superstitious prevision of success that he withdrew into the entry of the court.

The steps drew swiftly nearer, and swelled out suddenly louder as they turned the end of the street. The lawyer, looking forth from the entry, could soon see what manner of man he had to deal with. He was small and very plain-ly dressed, and the look of him, even at that distance, went somehow strongly against the watcher's inclination. But he made straight for the door, crossing the roadway to save time; and, as he came, he drew a key from his pocket, like one approaching home.

Mr. Utterson stepped out and touched him on the shoulder as he passed. "Mr. Hyde, I think?"

Mr. Hyde shrunk back with a hissing intake of the breath. But his fear was only momentary; and though he did not look the lawyer in the face, he answered coolly enough: "That is my name. What do you want?"

"I see you are going in," returned the lawyer. "I am an old friend of Dr. Jekyll's—Mr. Utterson, of Gaunt Street,—you must have heard my name; and meeting you so conveniently, I thought you might admit me."

"You will not find Dr. Jekyll; he is from home," replied Mr. Hyde, blowing in the key. And then suddenly, but still without looking up, "How did you know me?" he asked.

"On your side," said Mr. Utterson, "will you do me a favor?"

"With pleasure," replied the other. "What shall it be?"

"Will you let me see your face?" asked the lawyer.

Mr. Hyde appeared to hesitate, and then, as if upon some sudden reflection, fronted about with an air of defiance; and the pair stared at each other pretty fixedly for a few seconds. "Now I shall know you again," said Mr. Utterson. "It may be useful."

"Yes," returned Mr. Hyde, "It is as well we have met; and, *a propos,* you should have my address." And he gave a number of a street in Soho.

"Good God!" thought Mr. Utterson, "can he, too, have been thinking of the will?" But he kept his feelings to himself and only grunted in acknowledgment of the address.

"And now," said the other, "how did you know me?"

"By description," was the reply.

"Whose description?"

"We have common friends," said Mr. Utterson.

"Common friends?" echoed Mr. Hyde, a little hoarsely. "Who are they?"

"Jekyll, for instance," said the lawyer.

"He never told you," cried Mr. Hyde, with a flush of anger. "I did not think you would have lied."

"Come," said Mr. Utterson, "that is not fitting language."

The other snarled aloud into a savage laugh; and the next moment, with extraordinary quickness, he had unlocked the door and disappeared into the house.

The lawyer stood awhile when Mr. Hyde had left him, the picture of disquietude. Then he began slowly to mount the street, pausing every step or two and putting his hand to his brow like a man in mental perplexity. The problem he was thus debating as he walked, was one of a class that is rarely solved. Mr. Hyde was pale and dwarfish, he gave an impression of deformity without any namable malformation, he had a displeasing smile, he had borne himself to the lawyer with a sort of murderous mixture of timidity and boldness, and he spoke with a husky, whispering, and somewhat broken voice: all these were points against him, but not all of these together could explain the hitherto unknown disgust, loathing, and fear with which Mr. Utterson regarded him. "There must be something else," said the perplexed gentleman. "There is something more, if I could find a name for it. God bless me, the man seems hardly human! Something troglodytic, shall we say? or can it be the old story of Dr. Fell? or is it the mere radiance of a foul soul that thus transpires through, and transfigures, its clay continent? The last, I think; for oh, my poor old Harry Jekyll, if ever I read Satan's signature on a face, it is on that of your new friend."

Round the corner from the by-street there was a square of ancient, handsome houses, now for the most part decayed from their high estate and let in flats and chambers to all sorts and conditions of men: map-engravers, architects, shady lawyers, and the agents of obscure enterprises. One house, however, second from the corner, was still occupied entire; and at the door of this, which bore a great air of wealth and comfort, though it was now plunged in darkness except for the fanlight, Mr. Utterson stopped and knocked. A well-dressed, elderly servant opened the door.

"Is Dr. Jekyll at home, Poole?" asked the lawyer.

"I will see, Mr. Utterson," said Poole, admitting the

visitor, as he spoke, into a large, low-roofed, comfortable hall, paved with flags, warmed (after the fashion of a country-house) by a bright, open fire, and furnished with costly cabinets of oak. "Will you wait here by the fire, sir? or shall I give you a light in the dining-room?"

"Here, thank you," said the lawyer, and he drew near and leaned on the tall fender. This hall, in which he was now left alone, was a pet fancy of his friend the doctor's; and Utterson himself was wont to speak of it as the pleasantest room in London. But to-night there was a shudder in his blood; the face of Hyde sat heavy on his memory; he felt (what is rare with him) a nausea and distaste of life; and in the gloom of his spirits, he seemed to read a menace in the flickering of the firelight on the polished cabinets and the uneasy starting of the shadow on the roof. He was ashamed of his relief, when Poole presently returned to announce that Dr. Jekyll was gone out.

"I saw Mr. Hyde go in by the old dissecting-room door, Poole," he said. "Is that right, when Dr. Jekyll is from home?"

"Quite right, Mr. Utterson, sir," replied the servant. "Mr. Hyde has a key."

"Your master seems to repose a great deal of trust in that young man, Poole," resumed the other, musingly.

"Yes, sir, he do, indeed," said Poole. "We have all orders to obey him."

"I do not think I ever met Mr. Hyde?" asked Utterson.

"Oh, dear, no, sir. He never *dines* here," replied the butler. "Indeed, we see very little of him on this side of the house; he mostly comes and goes by the laboratory."

"Well, good-night, Poole."

"Good-night, Mr. Utterson."

And the lawyer set out homeward with a very heavy heart. "Poor Harry Jekyll," he thought, "my mind misgives me he is in deep waters! He was wild when he was young—a long while ago, to be sure; but in the law of God there is no statute of limitations. Ay, it must be that; the ghost of some old sin, the cancer of some concealed disgrace: punishment coming, *pede claudo*, years after memory has forgotten, and self-love condoned, the fault." And the lawyer, scared by the thought, brooded awhile on his own past, groping in all the corners of memory, lest, by chance, some Jack-in-the-box of an old iniquity should leap to light there. His past was fairly blameless; few men could read the rolls of their life with less apprehension; yet he was humbled to the dust by the many ill things he had done, and raised up again into a sober and fearful gratitude by the many that he had come so near to doing, yet avoided. And then, by a return on his former subject, he conceived a spark of hope. "This Master Hyde, if he were studied," thought he, "must have secrets of his own—black secrets, by the look of him; secrets compared to which poor Jekyll's worst would be like sunshine. Things cannot continue as they are. It turns me cold to think of this creature stealing like a thief to Harry's bedside; poor Harry, what a wakening! And the danger of it; for if this Hyde suspects the existence of the will, he may grow impatient to inherit! Ay, I must put my shoulder to the wheel, if Jekyll will but let me," he added, "if Jekyll will only let me." For once more he saw before his mind's eye, as clear as a transparency, the strange clauses of the will.

DR. JEKYLL WAS QUITE AT EASE

A FORTNIGHT later, by excellent good fortune, the doctor gave one of his pleasant dinners to some five or six old cronies, all intelligent, reputable men, and all judges of good wine; and Mr. Utterson so contrived that he remained behind after the others had departed. This was no new arrangement, but a thing that had befallen many scores of times. Where Utterson was liked, he was liked well. Hosts loved to detain the dry lawyer, when the light-hearted and the loose-tongued had already their foot on the threshold; they liked to sit awhile in his unobtrusive company, practicing for solitude, sobering their minds in the man's rich silence after the expense and strain of gayety. To this rule, Dr. Jekyll was no exception; and as he now sat on the opposite side of the fire— a large, well-made, smooth-faced man of fifty, with something of a slyish cast, perhaps, but every mark of capacity and kindness—you could see by his looks that he cherished for Mr. Utterson a sincere and warm affection.

"I have been wanting to speak to you, Jekyll," began the latter. "You know that will of yours?"

A close observer might have gathered that the topic was distasteful; but the doctor carried it off gayly. "My poor Utterson," said he, "you are unfortunate in such a client. I never saw a man so distressed as you were by my will; unless it were that hide-bound pedant, Lanyon, at what he called my scientific heresies. Oh, I know he's a good fellow—you needn't frown—an excellent fellow, and I always mean to see more of him; but a hide-bound pedant for all that; an ignorant, blatant pedant. I was never more disappointed in any man than Lanyon."

"You know I never approved of it," pursued Utterson, ruthlessly disregarding the fresh topic.

"My will? Yes, certainly, I know that," said the doctor, a trifle sharply. "You have told me so."

"Well, I tell you so again," continued the lawyer. "I have been learning something of young Hyde."

The large handsome face of Dr. Jekyll grew pale to the very lips, and there came a blackness about his eyes. "I do not care to hear more," said he. "This is a matter I thought we had agreed to drop."

"What I heard was abominable," said Utterson.

"It can make no change. You do not understand my position," returned the doctor, with a certain incoherency of manner. "I am painfully situated, Utterson; my position is a very strange—a very strange one. It is one of those affairs that cannot be mended by talking."

"Jekyll," said Utterson, "you know me; I am a man to be trusted. Make a clean breast of this in confidence; and I make no doubt I can get you out of it."

"My good Utterson," said the doctor, "this is very good of you; this is downright good of you, and I cannot find words to thank you in. I believe you fully; I would trust you before any man alive, ay, before myself, if I could make the choice; but indeed it isn't what you fancy; it is not so bad as that; and just to put your good heart at rest, I will tell you one thing; the moment I choose, I can be rid of Mr. Hyde. I give you my hand upon that; and I thank you again and again; and I will just add one little word,

Utterson, that I'm sure you'll take in good part; this is a private matter, and I beg of you to let it sleep."

Utterson reflected a little, looking into the fire.

"I have no doubt you are perfectly right," he said at last, getting to his feet.

"Well, but since we have touched upon this business, and for the last time I hope," continued the doctor, "there is one point I should like you to understand. I have really a very great interest in poor Hyde. I know you have seen him; he told me so; and I fear he was rude. But I do sincerely take a great, a very great interest in that young man; and if I am taken away, Utterson, I wish you to promise me that you will bear with him and get his rights for him. I think you would, if you knew all; and it would be a weight off my mind if you would promise."

"I can't pretend that I shall ever like him," said the lawyer.

"I don't ask that," pleaded Jekyll, laying his hand upon the other's arm; "I only ask for justice; I only ask you to help him for my sake, when I am no longer here."

Utterson heaved an irrepressible sigh. "Well," said he, "I promise."

THE CAREW MURDER CASE

NEARLY a year later, in the month of October, 18—, London was startled by a crime of singular ferocity, and rendered all the more notable by the high position of the victim. The details were few and startling. A maid-servant, living alone in a house not far from the river, had gone up-stairs to bed about eleven. Although a fog rolled over the city in the small hours, the early part of the night was cloudless, and the lane, which the maid's window overlooked, was brilliantly lit by the full moon. It seems she was romantically given, for she sat down upon her box, which stood immediately under the window, and fell into a dream of musing. Never (she used to say, with streaming tears, when she narrated that experience), never had she felt more at peace with all men or thought more kindly of the world. And as she so sat she became aware of an aged and beautiful gentleman with white hair, drawing near along the lane; and advancing to meet him, another and very small gentleman, to whom at first she paid less attention.

When they had come within speech (which was just under the maid's eyes) the older man bowed and accosted the other with a very pretty manner of politeness. It did not seem as if the subject of his address were of great importance; indeed, from his pointing, it sometimes appeared as if he were only inquiring his way; but the moon shone on his face as he spoke, and the girl was pleased to watch it, it seemed to breathe such an innocent and old-world kindness of disposition, yet with something high, too, as of a well-founded self-content. Presently her eyes wandered to the other, and she was surprised to recognize in him a certain Mr. Hyde, who had once visited her master and for whom she had conceived a dislike. He had in his hand a heavy cane, with which he was trifling; but he answered never a word, and seemed to listen with an ill-contained impatience. And then all of a sudden he broke out in a great flame of anger, stamping with his foot, brandishing the cane, and carrying on (as the maid described it) like a madman. The old gentleman took a step back with the air of one very much surprised and a trifle hurt; and at that Mr. Hyde broke out of all bounds and clubbed him to the earth. And next moment, with ape-like fury, he was trampling his victim under foot and hailing down a storm of blows, under which the bones were audibly shattered and the body jumped upon the roadway. At the horror of these sights and sounds, the maid fainted.

It was two o'clock when she came to herself and called for the police. The murderer was gone long ago; but there lay his victim in the middle of the lane, incredibly mangled. The stick with which the deed had been done, although it was of some rare and very tough and heavy wood, had broken in the middle under the stress of this insensate cruelty; and one splintered half had rolled in the neighboring gutter—the other, without doubt, had been carried away by the murderer. A purse and a gold watch were found upon the victim; but no cards or papers, except a sealed and stamped envelope, which he had been probably carrying to the post, and which bore the name and address of Mr. Utterson.

This was brought to the lawyer the next morning, before he was out of bed; and he had no sooner seen it, and been told the circumstances, than he shot out a solemn lip. "I shall say nothing till I have seen the body," said he; "this may be very serious. Have the kindness to wait while I dress." And with the same grave countenance he hurried through his breakfast and drove to the police station, whither the body had been carried. As soon as he came into the cell, he nodded.

"Yes," said he, "I recognize him. I am sorry to say that this is Sir Danvers Carew."

"Good God, sir," exclaimed the officer, "is it possible?" and the next moment his eye lighted up with professional ambition. "This will make a deal of noise," he said. "And perhaps you can help us to the man." And he briefly narrated what the maid had seen, and showed the broken stick.

Mr. Utterson had already quailed at the name of Hyde, but when the stick was laid before him, he could doubt no longer; broken and battered as it was, he recognized it for one that he had himself presented many years before to Henry Jekyll.

"Is this Mr. Hyde a person of small stature?" he inquired.

"Particularly small and particularly wicked-looking, is what the maid calls him," said the officer.

Mr. Utterson reflected; and then, raising his head, "If you will come with me in my cab," he said, "I think I can take you to his house."

It was by this time about nine in the morning, and the first fog of the season. A great chocolate colored pall lowered over heaven, but the wind was continually charging and routing these embattled vapors; so that as the cab crawled from street to street, Mr. Utterson beheld a marvelous number of degrees and hues of twilight; for here it would be dark like the black end of evening; and there would be a glow of a rich, lurid brown, like the light of some strange conflagration; and here, for a moment, the fog would be quite broken up, and a haggard shaft of daylight would glance in between the swirling wreaths. The dismal quarter of Soho seen under these changing glimpses, with its muddy ways, and slatternly passengers, and its lamps, which had never been extinguished or had been kindled afresh to combat this mournful reinvasion of darkness, seemed, in the lawyer's eyes, like a district of some city in a nightmare. The thoughts of his mind, besides, were of the gloomiest dye; and when he glanced at the companion of his drive, he was conscious of some touch of that terror of the law and the law's officers which may at times assail the most honest.

As the cab drew up before the address indicated, the fog lifted a little and showed him a dingy street, a gin-palace, a low French eating-house, a shop for the retail of penny numbers and twopenny salads, many ragged children huddled in the doorways, and many women of many different nationalities passing out, key in hand, to have a morning glass; and the next moment the fog settled down again upon that part, as brown as umber, and cut him off from his blackguardly surroundings. This was the home of Henry Jekyll's favorite; of a man who was heir to quarter of a million sterling.

An ivory-faced and silvery-haired old woman opened the door. She had an evil face, smoothed by hypocrisy, but her manners were excellent. Yes, she said, this was Mr. Hyde's, but he was not at home; he had been in that night very late, but had gone away again in less than an hour; there was nothing strange in that; his habits were very irregular, and he was often absent; for instance, it was nearly two months since she had seen him till yesterday.

"Very well, then, we wish to see his rooms," said the lawyer; and when the woman began to declare it was impossible, "I had better tell you who this person is," he added. "This is Inspector Newcomen of Scotland Yard."

A flash of odious joy appeared upon the woman's face. "Ah!" said she, "he is in trouble! What has he done?"

Mr. Utterson and the inspector exchanged glances. "He don't seem a very popular character," observed the latter. "And now, my good woman, just let me and this gentleman have a look about us."

In the whole extent of the house, which but for the old woman remained otherwise empty, Mr. Hyde had only used a couple of rooms; but these were furnished with luxury and good taste. A closet was filled with wine; the plate was of silver, the napery elegant; a good picture hung upon the walls, a gift (as Utterson supposed) from Henry Jekyll, who was much of a connoisseur; and the carpets were of many plies and agreeable in color. At this moment, however, the rooms bore every mark of having been recently and hurriedly ransacked; clothes lay about the floor, with their pockets inside out; lockfast drawers stood open; and on the hearth there lay a pile of gray ashes, as though many papers had been burned. From

these embers the inspector disinterred the butt-end of a
green check-book, which had resisted the action of the
fire; the other half of the stick was found behind the door;
and as this clinched his suspicions, the officer declared
himself delighted. A visit to the bank, where several thousand pounds were found to be lying to the murderer's
credit, completed his gratification.

"You may depend upon it, sir," he told Mr. Utterson:
"I have him in my hand. He must have lost his head, or
he never would have left the stick, or, above all, burned
the check-book. Why, money's life to the man. We have
nothing to do but wait for him at the bank, and get out
the handbills."

This last, however, was not so easy of accomplishment;
for Mr. Hyde had numbered few familiars—even the
master of the servant-maid had only seen him twice; his
family could nowhere be traced; he had never been
photographed; and the few who could describe him differed widely, as common observers will. Only on one point
were they agreed; and that was the haunting sense of unex-
pressed deformity with which the fugitive impressed his
beholders.

INCIDENT OF THE LETTER

IT was late in the afternoon when Mr. Utterson found his way to Dr. Jekyll's door, where he was at once admitted by Poole, and carried down by the kitchen offices and across a yard which had once been a garden, to the building which was indifferently known as the laboratory or the dissecting rooms. The doctor had bought the house from the heirs of a celebrated surgeon; and his own tastes being rather chemical than anatomical, had changed the destination of the block at the bottom of the garden.

It was the first time that the lawyer had been received in that part of his friend's quarters; and he eyed the dingy, windowless structure with curiosity, and gazed round with a distasteful sense of strangeness as he crossed the theater, once crowded with eager students, and now lying gaunt and silent, the tables laden with chemical apparatus, the floor strewn with crates and littered with packing straw, and the light falling dimly through the foggy cupola. At the further end, a flight of stairs mounted to a door covered with red baize; and through this Mr. Utterson was at last received into the doctor's cabinet. It was a large room, fitted round with glass presses, furnished, among other things, with a cheval glass and a business table, and looking out upon the court by three dusty windows barred with iron. The fire burned in the grate; a lamp was set lighted on the chimney shelf, for even in the houses the fog began to lie thickly; and there, close up to the warmth, sat Dr. Jekyll, looking deadly sick. He did not rise to meet his visitor, but held out a cold hand and bade him welcome in a changed voice.

"And now," said Mr. Utterson, as soon as Poole had left them, "you have heard the news?"

The doctor shuddered. "They were crying it in the square," he said. "I heard them in my dining-room."

"One word," said the lawyer. "Carew was my client, but so are you, and I want to know what I am doing. You have not been mad enough to hide this fellow?"

"Utterson, I swear to God," cried the doctor, "I swear to God I will never set eyes on him again. I bind my honor to you that I am done with him in this world. It is all at an end. And indeed he does not want my help; you do not know him as I do; he is safe, he is quite safe; mark my words, he will never more be heard of."

The lawyer listened gloomily; he did not like his friend's feverish manner. "You seem pretty sure of him," said he; "and for your sake, I hope you may be right. If it came to a trial, your name might appear."

"I am quite sure of him," replied Jekyll; "I have grounds for certainty that I cannot share with any one. But there is one thing on which you may advise me. I have—I have received a letter, and I am at a loss whether I should show it to the police. I should like to leave it in your hands, Utterson; you would judge wisely I am sure; I have so great a trust in you."

"You fear, I suppose, that it might lead to his detection?" asked the lawyer.

"No," said the other. "I cannot say that I care what becomes of Hyde; I am quite done with him. I was thinking of my own character, which this hateful business has rather exposed."

Utterson ruminated awhile; he was surprised at his friend's selfishness, and yet relieved by it. "Well," said he, at last, "let me see the letter."

The letter was written in an odd, upright hand, and signed "Edward Hyde;" and it signified briefly enough, that the writer's benefactor, Dr. Jekyll, whom he had long so unworthily repaid for a thousand generosites, need labor under no alarm for his safety, as he had means of escape on which he placed a sure dependence. The lawyer liked this letter well enough; it put a better color on the intimacy than he had looked for; and he blamed himself for some of his past suspicions.

"Have you the envelope?" he asked.

"I buraned it," replied Jekyll, "before I thought what I was about. But it bore no postmark. The note was handed in."

"Shall I keep this and sleep upon it?" asked Utterson.

"I wish you to judge for me entirely," was the reply. "I have lost confidence in myself."

"Well, I shall consider," returned the lawyer. "And now one word more: it was Hyde who dictated the terms in your will about that disappearance?"

The doctor seemed seized with a qualm of faintness; he shut his mouth tight and nodded.

"I knew it," said Utterson. "He meant to murder you. You have had a fine escape."

"I have had what is far more to the purpose," returned the doctor, solemnly; "I have had a lesson—oh, God, Utterson, what a lesson I have had!" And he covered his face for a moment with his hands.

On his way out, the lawyer stopped and had a word or two with Poole. "By the bye," said he, "there was a letter handed in to-day; what was the messenger like?" But Poole was positive nothing had come except by post; "and only circulars by that," he added.

This news sent off the visitor with his fears renewed. Plainly the letter had come by the laboratory door; possibly, indeed, it had been written in the cabinet; and if that were so, it must be differently judged, and handled with the more caution. The newsboys, as he went, were crying themselves hoarse along the footways: "Special edition. Shocking murder of an M. P." That was the funeral oration of one friend and client; and he could not help a certain apprehension lest the good name of another should be sucked down in the eddy of the scandal. It was, at least, a ticklish decision that he had to make; and self-reliant as he was by habit, he began to cherish a longing for advice. It was not to be had directly; but perhaps, he thought, it might be fished for.

Presently after, he sat on one side of his own hearth, with Mr. Guest, his head clerk, upon the other, and midway between, at a nicely calculated distance from the fire, a bottle of a particular old wine that had long dwelt unsunned in the foundations of his house. The fog still slept on the wing above the drowned city, where the lamps glimmered like carbuncles; and through the muffle and smother of these fallen clouds, the procession of the town's life was still rolling in through the great arteries with a sound as of a mighty wind. But the room was gay with firelight. In the bottle the acids were long ago resolved; the imperial dye had softened with time, as the color grows richer in stained windows; and the glow of hot au-

tumn afternoons on hill-side vineyards was ready to be
set free and to disperse the fogs of London. Insensibly
the lawyer melted. There was no man from whom he kept
fewer secrets than Mr. Guest; and he was not always sure
that he kept as many as he meant. Guest had often been
on business to the doctor's; he knew Poole; he could scarce
have failed to hear of Mr. Hyde's familiarity about the
house, he might draw conclusions; was it not as well, then,
that he should see a letter which put that mystery to rights?
and above all since Guest, being a great student and critic
of handwriting, would consider the step natural and oblig-
ing? The clerk, besides, was a man of counsel; he would
scarce read so strange a document without dropping a remark; and by that remark Mr. Utterson might shape his
future course.

"This is sad business about Sir Danvers," he said.

"Yes, sir, indeed. It has elicited a great deal of public
feeling," returned Guest. "The man, of course, was mad."

"I should like to hear your views on that," replied Utterson. "I have a document here in his handwriting; it
is between ourselves, for I scarce know what to do about
it; it is an ugly business at the best. But there it is;
quite in your way; a murderer's autograph."

Guest's eyes brightened, and he sat down at once and
studied it with passion. "No sir," he said; "not mad;
but it is an odd hand."

"And by all accounts a very odd writer," added the
lawyer.

Just then the servant entered with a note.

"Is that from Dr. Jekyll, sir?" inquired the clerk. "I
thought I knew the writing. Anything private, Mr. Utterson?"

"Only an invitation to dinner. Why? do you want to see it?"

"One moment. I thank you, sir;" and the clerk laid the two sheets of paper alongside and sedulously compared their contents. "Thank you, sir," he said at last, returning both; "it's a very interesting autograph."

There was a pause, during which Mr. Utterson struggled with himself. "Why did you compare them, Guest?" he inquired, suddenly.

"Well, sir," returned the clerk, "there's a rather singular resemblance; the two hands are in many points identical; only differently sloped."

"Rather quaint," said Utterson.

"It is, as you say, rather quaint," returned Guest.

"I wouldn't speak of this note, you know," said the master.

"No, sir," said the clerk. "I understand."

But no sooner was Mr. Utterson alone that night, than he locked the note into his safe, where it reposed from that time forward. "What!" he thought. "Henry Jekyll forge for a murderer!" And his blood ran cold in his veins.

REMARKABLE INCIDENT OF DOCTOR LANYON

TIME ran on; thousands of pounds were offered in reward, for the death of Sir Danvers was resented as a public injury; but Mr. Hyde had disappeared out of the ken of the police as though he had never existed. Much of his past was unearthed, indeed, and all disreputable; tales came out of the man's cruelty, at once so callous and violent, of his vile life, of his strange associates, of the hatred that seemed to have surrounded his career; but of his present whereabouts, not a whisper. From the time he had left the house in Soho on the morning of the murder, he was simply blotted out; and gradually, as time grew on, Mr. Utterson began to recover from the hotness of his alarm, and to grow more at quiet with himself. The death of Sir Danvers was, to his way of thinking, more than paid for by the disappearance of Mr. Hyde. Now that that evil influence had been withdrawn, a new life began for Dr. Jekyll. He came out of his seclusion, renewed relations with his friends, became once more their familiar guest and entertainer; and whilst he had always been known for charities, he was now no less distinguished for religion. He was busy, he was much in the open air, he did good; his face seemed to open and brighten, as if with an inward consciousness of service; and for more than two months the doctor was at peace.

On the 8th of January, Utterson had dined at the doctor's with a small party; Lanyon had been there; and

the face of the host had looked from one to the other as
in the old days when the trio were inseparable friends.
On the 12th, and again on the 14th, the door was shut
against the lawyer. "The doctor was confined to the
house," Poole said, "and saw no one." On the 15th, he
tried again, and was again refused; and having now been
used for the last two months to see his friend almost
daily, he found this return of solitude to weigh upon his
spirits. The fifth night, he had in Guest to dine with
him; and the sixth he betook himself to Dr. Lanyon's.

There at least he was not denied admittance; but when
he came in, he was shocked at the change that had taken
place in the doctor's appearance. He had his death-
warrent written legibly upon his face. The rosy man had
grown pale; his flesh had fallen away; he was visibly
balder and older; and yet it was not so much these tokens
of a swift physical decay that arrested the lawyer's notice,
as a look in the eye and quality of manner that seemed
to testify to some deep-seated terror of the mind. It was
unlikely that the doctor should fear death; and yet that
was what Utterson was tempted to suspect. "Yes," he
thought; "he is a doctor, he must know his own state and
that his days are counted; and the knowledge is more than
he can bear." And yet when Utterson remarked on his
ill-looks, it was with an air of great firmness that Lanyon
declared himself a doomed man.

"I have had a shock," he said, "and I shall never recover. It is a question of weeks. Well, life has been pleasant; I liked it; yes, sir, I used to like it. I sometimes
think, if we knew all, we should be more glad to get
away."

"Jekyll is ill, too," observed Utterson. "Have you seen him?"

But Lanyon's face changed, and he held up a trembling hand. "I wish to see or hear no more of Doctor Jekyll," he said, in a low, unsteady voice. "I am quite done with that person; and I beg that you will spare me any allusion to one whom I regard as dead."

"Tut-tut," said Mr. Utterson; and then, after a considerable pause, "Can I do anything?" he inquired. "We are three very old friends, Lanyon; we shall not live to make others."

"Nothing can be done," returned Lanyon; "ask himself."

"He will not see me," said the lawyer.

"I am not surprised at that," was the reply. "Some day, Utterson, after I am dead, you may perhaps come to learn the right and wrong of this. I cannot tell you. And in the meantime, if you can sit and talk with me of other things, for God's sake, stay and do so; but if you cannot keep clear of this accursed topic, then, in God's name, go, for I cannot bear it."

As soon as he got home, Utterson sat down and wrote to Jekyll, complaining of his exclusion from the house, and asking the cause of this unhappy break with Lanyon; and the next day brought him a long answer, often very pathetically worded, and sometimes darkly mysterious in drift. The quarrel with Lanyon was incurable. "I do not blame our old friend," Jekyll wrote, "but I share his view that we must never meet. I mean from henceforth to lead a life of extreme seclusion; you must not be surprised, nor must you doubt my friendship, if my door is often shut even to you. You must suffer me to go my own dark way. I have brought on myself a punishment and a danger that I cannot name. If I am the chief of sinners, I am the chief of sufferers also. I could not think that this earth contained a place for sufferings and terrors so unmanning; and you can do but one thing, Utterson, to lighten this destiny, and that is to respect my silence."

Utterson was amazed; the dark influence of Hades had been withdrawn, the doctor had returned to his old tasks and amities; a week ago, the prospect had smiled with every promise of a cheerful and an honored age; and now in a moment, friendship, and peace of mind, and the whole tenor of his life were wrecked. So great and unprepared a change pointed to madness: but in view of Lanyon's manner and words, there must lie for it some deeper ground.

A week afterward Dr. Lanyon took to his bed, and in something less than a fortnight he was dead. The night after the funeral, at which he had been sadly affected, Utterson locked the door of his business room, and sitting there by the light of a melancholy candle, drew out and set before him an envelope addressed by the hand and sealed with the seal of his dead friend. "PRIVATE: for the hands of J. G. UTTERSON ALONE, and in case of his predecease *to be destroyed unread,*" so it was emphatically superscribed; and the lawyer dreaded to behold the contents. "I have buried one friend to-day," he thought; "what if this should cost me another?" And then he condemned the fear as a disloyalty, and broke the seal. Within there was another inclosure, likewise sealed, and marked upon the cover as "not to be opened till the death or disappearance of Dr. Henry Jekyll." Utterson could not trust his eyes. Yes, it was disappearance; here again, as in the mad will which he had long ago restored to its author, here again were the idea of a disappearance and the name of Henry Jekyll bracketed. But in the will, the idea had sprung from the sinister suggestion of the man Hyde; it was set there with a purpose all too plain and horrible. Written by the hand of Lanyon, what should it mean? A great curiosity came on the trustee, to disregard the prohibition and dive at once to the bottom of these mysteries; but professional honor and faith to his dead friend were stringent obligations; and the packet slept in the inmost corner of his private safe.

It is one thing to mortify curiosity, another to conquer it; and it may be doubted if, from that day forth, Utterson desired the society of his surviving friend with the same eagerness. He thought of him kindly; but his thoughts were disquieted and fearful. He went to call indeed; but he was perhaps relieved to be denied admittance; perhaps, in his heart, he desired to speak with Poole upon the doorstep and surrounded by the air and sounds of the open city, rather than to be admitted into that house of voluntary bondage, and to sit and speak with its inscrutable recluse. Poole had, indeed, no very pleasant news to communicate. The doctor, it appeared, now more than ever confined himself to the cabinet over the laboratory, where he would sometimes even sleep; he was out of spirits, he had grown very silent, he did not read; it seemed as if he had something on his mind. Utterson became so used to the unvarying character of these reports, that he fell off little by little in the frequency of his visits.

INCIDENT AT THE WINDOW

IT chanced on Sunday, when Mr. Utterson was on his usual walk with Mr. Enfield, that their way lay once again through the by-street; and that when they came in front of the door, both stopped to gaze on it.

"Well," said Enfield, "that story's at an end at least. We shall never see more of Mr. Hyde."

"I hope not," said Utterson. "Did I ever tell you that I once saw him, and shared your feeling of repulsion?"

"It was impossible to do the one with the other," returned Enfield. "And by the way, what an ass you must have thought me, not to know that this was a back way to Dr. Jekyll's! It was partly your own fault that I found it out, even when I did."

"So you found it, did you?" said Utterson. "But if that be so, we may step into the court and take a look at the windows. To tell you the truth, I am uneasy about poor Jekyll; and even outside, I feel as if the presence of a friend might do him good."

The court was very cool and a little damp, and full of premature twilight, although the sky high up overhead, was still bright with sunset. The middle one of the three windows was half way open, and sitting close beside it, taking the air with an infinite sadness of mien, like some disconsolate prisoner, Utterson saw Dr. Jekyll.

"What! Jekyll!" he cried. "I trust you are better."

"I am very low, Utterson," replied the doctor, drearily, "very low. It will not last long, thank God."

"You stay too much in-doors," said the lawyer. "You should be out whipping up the circulation like Mr. Enfield and me. (This is my cousin—Mr. Enfield—Dr. Jekyll.) Come now; get your hat and take a quick turn with us."

"You are very good," sighed the other. "I should like to very much; but no, no, no, it is quite impossible; I dare not. But indeed, Utterson, I am very glad to see you: this is really a great pleasure; I would ask you and Mr. Enfield up, but the place is really not fit."

"Why, then," said the lawyer, good-naturedly, "the best thing we can do is to stay down here and speak with you from where we are."

"That is just what I was about to venture to propose," returned the doctor with a smile. But the words were hardly uttered, before the smile was struck out of his face and succeeded by an expression of such abject terror and despair, as froze the very blood of the two gentlemen below. They saw it but for a glimpse, for the window was instantly thrust down; but that glimpse had been sufficient, and they turned and left the court without a word. In silence, too, they traversed the by-street; and it was not until they had come into a neighboring thoroughfare, where even upon a Sunday there were still some stirrings of life, that Mr. Utterson at last turned and looked at his companion. They were both pale; and there was an answering look of horror in their eyes.

"God forgive us, God forgive us," said Mr. Utterson.

But Mr. Enfield only nodded his head very seriously, and walked on once more in silence.

THE LAST NIGHT

MR. UTTERSON was sitting by his fireside one evening after dinner, when he was surprised to receive a visit from Poole.

"Bless me, Poole, what brings you here?" he cried; and then taking a second look at him, "What ails you?" he added, "is the doctor ill?"

"Mr. Utterson," said the man, "there is something wrong."

"Take a seat, and here is a glass of wine for you," said the lawyer. "Now, take your time, and tell me plainly what you want."

"You know the doctor's ways, sir," replied Poole, "and how he shuts himself up. Well, he's shut up again in the cabinet; and I don't like it, sir—I wish I may die if I like it. Mr. Utterson, sir, I'm afraid."

"Now, my good man," said the lawyer, "be explicit. What are you afraid of?"

"I've been afraid for about a week," returned Poole, doggedly disregarding the question, "and I can bear it no more."

The man's appearance amply bore out his words, his manner was altered for the worse; and, except for the moment when he had first announced his terror, he had not once looked the lawyer in the face. Even now, he sat with the glass of wine untasted on his knee, and his eyes directed to a corner of the floor. "I can bear it no more," he repeated.

"Come," said the lawyer, "I see you have some good reason, Poole; I see there is something seriously amiss. Try to tell me what it is."

"I think there has been foul play," said Poole, hoarsely.

"Foul play!" cried the lawyer, a good deal frightened and rather inclined to be irritated in consequence. "What foul play? What does the man mean?"

"I daren't say, sir," was the answer; "but will you come along with me and see for yourself?"

Mr. Utterson's only answer was to rise and get his hat and great coat; but he observed with wonder the greatness of the relief that appeared upon the butler's face, and, per-haps with no less, that the wine was still untasted when he set it down to follow.

It was a wild, cold, seasonable night of March, with a pale moon, lying on her back, as though the wind had tilted her, and a flying wrack of the most diaphanous and lawny texture. The wind made talking difficut, and fleck-ed the blood into the face. It seemed to have swept the streets unusually bare of passengers, besides; for Mr. Ut-terson thought he had never seen that part of London so deserted. He could have wished it otherwise; never in his life had he been conscious of so sharp a wish to see and touch his fellow-creatures; for, struggle as he might, there was borne in upon his mind a crushing anticipation of calamity. The square, when they got there, was all full of wind and dust, and the thin trees in the garden were lashing themselves along the railing. Poole, who had kept all the way a pace or two ahead, now pulled up in the middle of the pavement, and in spite of the biting

weather, took off his hat and mopped his brow with a red
pocket-handkerchief. But for all the hurry of his coming,
these were not the dews of exertion that he wiped away,
but the moisture of some strangling anguish; for his face
was white, and his voice, when he spoke, harsh and
broken.

"Well, sir," he said, "here we are, and God grant there
be nothing wrong."

"Amen, Poole," said the lawyer.

Thereupon the servant knocked in a very guarded manner; the door was opened on the chain; and a voice asked
from within, "Is that you, Poole?"

"It's all right," said Poole. "Open the door."

The hall, when they entered it, was brightly lighted up,
the fire was built high; and about the hearth the whole of
the servants, men and women, stood huddled together like
a flock of sheep. At the sight of Mr. Utterson, the household broke into hysterical whimpering; and the cook, crying out, "Bless God! it's Mr. Utterson," ran forward as if
to take him in her arms.

"What, what? Are you all here?" said the lawyer,
peevishly. "Very irregular, very unseemly; your master
would be far from pleased."

"They're all afraid," said Poole.

Blank silence followed, no one protesting; only the maid
lifted up her voice and now wept loudly.

"Hold your tongue!" Poole said to her, with a ferocity
of accent that testified to his own jangled nerves; and indeed, when the girl had so suddenly raised the note of her
lamentation, they had all started and turned toward the
inner door with faces of dreadful expectation. "And
now," continued the butler, addressing the knife-boy,

"reach me a candle, and we'll get this through hands at once." And then he begged Mr. Utterson to follow him, and led the way to the back garden.

"Now, sir," said he, "you come as gently as you can. I want you to hear, and I don't want you to be heard. And see here, sir, if by any chance he was to ask you in, don't go."

Mr. Utterson's nerves, at this unlooked-for termination, gave a jerk that nearly threw him from his balance; but he recollected his courage and followed the butler into the laboratory building and through the surgical theater, with its lumber of crates and bottles, to the foot of the stair. Here Poole motioned him to stand on one side and listen; while he himself, setting down the candle and making a great and obvious call on his resolution, mounted the steps and knocked with a somewhat uncertain hand on the red baize of the cabinet door.

"Mr. Utterson, sir, asking to see you," he called; and even as he did so, once more violently signed to the lawyer to give ear.

A voice answered from within: "Tell him I cannot see any one," it said complainingly.

"Thank you, sir," said Poole, with a note of something like triumph in his voice: and taking up his candle, he led Mr. Utterson back across the yard and into the great kitchen, where the fire was out and the beetles were leaping on the floor.

"Sir," he said, looking Mr. Utterson in the eyes, "was that my master's voice?"

"It seems much changed," replied the lawyer, very pale, but giving look for look.

"Changed? Well, yes, I think so," said the butler.

"Have I been twenty years in this man's house, to be deceived about his voice? No, sir; master's made away with; he was made away with, eight days ago, when we heard him cry out upon the name of God; and *who's* in there instead of him, and *why* it stays there, is a thing that cries to Heaven, Mr. Utterson!"

"This is a very strange tale, Poole; this is rather a wild tale, my man," said Mr. Utterson, biting his finger. "Suppose it were as you suppose, supposing Dr. Jekyll to have been—well, murdered, what would induce the murderer to stay? That won't hold water; it doesn't commend itself to reason."

"Well, Mr. Utterson, you are a hard man to satisfy, but I'll do it yet," said Poole. "All this last week (you must know) him, or it, or whatever it is that lives in that cabinet, has been crying, night and day, for some sort of medicine, and cannot get it to his mind. It was sometimes his way—the master's, that is—to write his orders on a sheet of paper, and throw it on the stair. We've had nothing else this week back; nothing but papers, and a closed door, and the very meals left there to be smuggled in when nobody was looking. Well, sir, every day, ay, and twice and thrice in the same day, there have been orders and complaints, and I have been sent flying to all the wholesale chemists in town. Every time I brought the stuff back, there would be another paper telling me to return it, because it was not pure, and another order to a different firm. This drug is wanted bitter bad, sir, whatever for."

"Have you any of these papers?" asked Mr. Utterson.

Poole felt in his pocket, and handed out a crumpled note, which the lawyer, bending nearer to the candle, care-

fully examined. Its contents ran thus: "Dr. Jekyll pre-
sents his compliments to Messrs. Maw. He assures them
that their last sample is impure and quite useless for his
present purpose. In the year 18—, Dr. J. purchased a
somewhat large quantity from Messrs. M. He now begs
them to search with the most sedulous care, and should
any of the same quality be left, to forward it to him at
once. Expense is no consideration. The importance of
this to Dr. J. can hardly be exaggerated." So far the letter
had run composedly enough, but here, with a sudden
splutter of the pen, the writer's emotion had broken loose.
"For God's sake," he added, "find me some of the old."

"This is a strange note," said Mr. Utterson; and then
sharply, "How do you come to have it open?"

"The man at Maw's was main angry, sir, and he threw
it back to me like so much dirt," returned Poole.

"This is unquestionably the doctor's hand, do you
know?" resumed the lawyer.

"I thought it looked like it," said the servant rather
sulkily; and then, with another voice, "But what matters
hand of write," he said. "I've seen him!"

"Seen him?" repeated Mr. Utterson. "Well?"

"That's it!" said Poole. "It was this way. I came suddenly into the theater from the garden. It seems he had
slipped out to look for this drug or whatever it is; for
the cabinet door was open, and there he was at the far end
of the room digging among the crates. He looked up
when I came in, gave a kind of cry, and whipped up-stairs
into the cabinet. It was but for one minute that I saw
him, but the hair stood upon my head like quills. Sir, if
that was my master, why had he a mask upon his face?
If it was my master, why did he cry out like a rat, and run

from me? I have served him long enough. And then——"
the man paused and passed his hand over his face.

"These are all very strange circumstances," said Mr.
Utterson, "but I think I begin to see daylight. Your master, Poole, is plainly seized with one of those maladies that
both torture and deform the sufferer; hence, for aught I
know, the alteration of his voice; hence the mask and the
avoidance of his friends; hence his eagerness to find this
drug, by means of which the poor soul retains some hope
of ultimate recovery—God grant that he be not deceived!
There is my explanation; it is sad enough, Poole, ay,
and appalling to consider; but it is plain and natural,
hangs well together, and delivers us from all exorbitant
alarms."

"Sir," said the butler, turning to a sort of mottled pallor, "that thing was not my master, and there's the truth.
My master"—here he looked round him and began to
whisper—"is a tall fine build of a man and this was more
of a dwarf." Utterson attempted to protest. "Oh, sir,"
cried Poole, "do you think I do not know my master after
twenty year? Do you think I do not know where his head
comes to in the cabinet door, where I saw him every
morning of my life? No, sir, that thing in the mask was
never Doctor Jekyll—God knows what it was, but it was
never Doctor Jekyll; and it is the belief of my heart that
there was murder done."

"Poole," replied the lawyer, "if you say that, it will become my duty to make certain. Much as I desire to spare
your master's feelings, much as I am puzzled by this note
which seems to prove him to be still alive, I shall consider
it my duty to break in that door."

"Ah, Mr. Utterson, that's talking!" cried the butler.

"And now comes the second question," resumed Utterson: "Who is going to do it?"

"Why, you and me," was the undaunted reply.

"That's very well said," returned the lawyer; "and whatever comes of it, I shall make it my business to see you are no loser."

"There is an ax in the theater," continued Poole; "and you might take the kitchen poker for yourself."

The lawyer took that rude but weighty instrument into his hand, and balanced it. "Do you know, Poole," he said, looking up, "that you and I are about to place ourselves in a position of some peril?"

"You may say so, sir, indeed," returned the butler.

"It is well, then, that we should be frank," said the other. "We both think more than we have said; let us make a clean breast. This masked figure that you saw, did you recognize it?"

"Well, sir, it went so quick, and the creature was so doubled up, that I could hardly swear to that," was the answer. "But if you mean, was it Mr. Hyde?—why, yes, I think it was! You see, it was much of the same bigness; and it had the same quick light way with it; and then who else could have got in by the laboratory door? You have not forgot, sir, that at the time of the murder he had still the key with him? But that's not all. I don't know, Mr. Utterson, if ever you met this Mr. Hyde?"

"Yes," said the lawyer, "I once spoke with him."

"Then you must know as well as the rest of us that there was something queer about that gentleman—something that gave a man a turn—I don't know rightly how to say, sir, beyond this: that you felt it in your marrow kind of cold and thin."

"I own I felt something of what you describe," said Mr. Utterson.

"Quite so, sir," returned Poole. "Well, when that masked thing like a monkey jumped from among the chemicals and whipped into the cabinet, it went down my spine like ice. Oh, I know it's not evidence, Mr. Utterson; I'm book-learned enough for that; but a man has his feelings, and I give you my Bible word it was Mr. Hyde!"

"Ay, ay," said the lawyer. "My fears incline to the same point. Evil, I fear, founded—evil was sure to come—of that connection. Ay, truly, I believe you; I believe poor Harry is killed; and I believe his murderer (for what purpose, God alone can tell) is still lurking in his victim's room. Well, let our name be vengeance. Call Bradshaw."

The footman came at the summons, very white and nervous.

"Pull yourself together, Bradshaw,'" said the lawyer. "This suspense, I know, is telling upon all of you; but it is now our intention to make an end of it. Poole, here, and I are going to force our way into the cabinet. If all is well, my shoulders are broad enough to bear the blame. Meanwhile, lest anything should really be amiss, or any malefactor seek to escape by the back, you and the boy must go round the corner with a pair of good sticks, and take your post at the laboratory door. We give you ten minutes to get to your stations"

As Bradshaw left, the lawyer looked at his watch. "And now, Poole, let us get to ours," he said; and taking the poker under his arm, led the way into the yard. The scud had banked over the moon, and it was now quite dark. The wind, which only broke in puffs and draughts into that deep well of building, tossed the light of the candle to and fro about their steps, until they came into the shelter of the theater, where they sat down silently to wait. London hummed solemnly all around; but nearer at hand, the stillness was only broken by the sounds of a footfall moving to and fro along the cabinet floor.

"So it will walk all day, sir," whispered Poole; "ay, and the better part of the night. Only when a new sample comes from the chemist there's a bit of a break. Ah, it's an ill conscience that's such an enemy to rest! Ah, sir, there's blood foully shed in every step of it! But hark again, a little closer—put your heart in your ears, Mr. Utterson, and tell me, is that the doctor's foot?"

The steps fell lightly and oddly, with a certain swing, for all they went so slowly; it was different indeed from the heavy creaking tread of Henry Jekyll. Utterson sighed. "Is there never anything else?" he asked.

Poole nodded. "Once," he said. "Once I heard it weeping!"

"Weeping? how's that?" said the lawyer, conscious of a sudden thrill of horror.

"Weeping like a woman or a lost soul," said the butler. "I came away with that upon my heart, that I could have wept too."

But now the ten minutes drew to an end. Poole disinterred the ax from under a stack of packing-straw; the candle was set upon the nearest table to light them to the attack; and they drew near with bated breath to where that patient foot was still going up and down, up and down, in the quiet of the night.

"Jekyll," cried Utterson, with a loud voice, "I demand to see you." He paused a moment, but there came no reply. "I give you fair warning, our suspicions are aroused, and I must and shall see you," he resumed; "if not by fair means, then by foul—if not of your consent, then by brute force!"

"Utterson," said the voice, "for God's sake, have mercy!"

"Ah, that's not Jekyll's voice—it's Hyde's!" cried Utterson. "Down with the door, Poole."

Poole swung the ax over his shoulder; the blow shook the building, and the red baize door leaped against the lock and hinges. A dismal screech, as of mere animal terror, rang from the cabinet. Up went the ax again, and again the panels crashed and the frame bounded; four times the blow fell; but the wood was tough and the fittings were of excellent workmanship; and it was not until the fifth that the lock burst in sunder and the wreck of the door fell inward on the carpet.

The besiegers, appalled by their own riot and the stillness that succeeded, stood back a little and peered in. There lay the cabinet before their eyes in the quiet lamplight, a good fire glowing and chattering on the hearth, the kettle singing its thin strain, a drawer or two open, papers neatly set forth on the business table, and nearer the fire, the things laid out for tea; the quietest room, you would have said, and, but for the glazed presses full of chemicals, the most commonplace that night in London.

Right in the midst there lay the body of a man, sorely contorted and still twitching. They drew near on tiptoe, turned it on its back and beheld the face of Edward Hyde. He was dressed in clothes far too large for him, clothes of the doctor's bigness; the cords of his face still moved with a semblance of life, but life was quite gone; and by the crushed vial in his hand and the strong smell of kernels that hung upon the air, Utterson knew he was look-ing on the body of a self-destroyer.

"We have come too late," he said, sternly, "whether to save or punish. Hyde is gone to his account; and it only remains for us to find the body of your master."

The far greater porportion of the building was occu-pied by the theater, which filled almost the whole ground story and was lighted from above, and by the cabinet, which formed an upper story at one end and looked upon the court. A corridor joined the theater to the door on the by-street, and with this the cabinet communicated separately by a second flight of stairs. There were besides a few dark closets and a spacious cellar. All these they now thoroughly examined. Each closet needed but a glance, for all were empty, and all, by the dust that fell from their doors, had stood long unopened. The cellar, indeed, was filled with crazy lumber, mostly dating from the times of the surgeon who was Jekyll's predecessor; but even as they opened the door they were advertised of the usefulness of further search, by the fall of a perfect mat of cobweb which had for years sealed up the entrance. No-where was there any trace of Henry Jekyll, dead or alive.

Poole stamped on the flags of the corridor. "He must be buried here," he said, hearkening to the sound.

"Or he may have fled," said Utterson, and he turned to examine the door in the by-street. It was locked; and ly-ing near by on the flags, they found the key, already stain-ed with rust.

"This does not look like use," observed the lawyer.

"Use!" echoed Poole. "Do you not see, sir, it is broken? much as if a man had stamped on it."

"Ay," continued Utterson, "and the fractures, too, are

rusty." The two men looked at each other with a stare. "This is beyond me, Poole," said the lawyer. "Let us go back to the cabinet."

They mounted the stair in silence, and still with an occasional awe-struck glance at the dead body, proceeded more thoroughly to examine the contents of the cabinet. At one table, there were traces of chemical work, various measured heaps of some white salt being laid on glass saucers, as though for an experiment in which the unhappy man had been prevented.

"That is the same drug that I was always bringing him," said Poole; and even as he spoke, the kettle with a startling noise boiled over.

This brought them to the fireside, where the easy-chair was drawn cozily up, and the tea things stood ready to the sitter's elbow, the very sugar in the cup. There were several books on a shelf; one lay beside the tea things open, and Utterson was amazed to find it a copy of a pious work, for which Jekyll had several times expressed a great esteem, annotated, in his own hand, with startling blasphemies.

Next, in the course of their review of the chamber, the searchers came to the cheval-glass, into whose depths they looked with an involuntary horror. But it was so turned as to show them nothing but the rosy glow playing on the roof, the fire sparkling in a hundred repetitions along the glazed front of the presses, and their own pale and fearful countenances stooping to look in.

"This glass has seen some strange things, sir," whispered Poole.

"And surely none stranger than itself," echoed the lawyer in the same tones. "For what did Jekyll"—he caught himself up at the word with a start, and then conquering the weakness; "what could Jekyll want with it?" he said.

"You may say that!" said Poole.

Next they turned to the business-table. On the desk among the neat array of papers, a large envelope was uppermost, and bore, in the doctor's hand, the name of Mr. Utterson. The lawyer unsealed it, and several inclosures fell to the floor. The first was a will, drawn in the same eccentric terms as the one which he had returned six months before, to serve as a testament in case of death and as a deed of gift in case of disappearance; but in place of the name of Edward Hyde, the lawyer, with indescribable amazement, read the name of Gabriel John Utterson. He looked at Poole, and then back at the paper, and last of all at the dead malefactor stretched upon the carpet.

"My head goes round," he said. "He has been all these days in possession; he had no cause to like me; he must have raged to see himself displaced; and he has not destroyed this document."

He caught up the next paper; it was a brief note in the doctor's hand and dated at the top. "O Poole!" the lawyer cried, "he was alive and here this day. He cannot have been disposed of in so short a space, he must be still alive, he must have fled! And then, why fled? and how? and in that case, can we venture to declare this suicide? O, we must be careful. I foresee that we may yet involve your master in some dire catastrophe."

"Why don't you read it, sir?" asked Poole.

"Because I fear," replied the lawyer solemnly; "God grant I have no cause for it!" And with that he brought the paper to his eyes and read as follows:

"MY DEAR UTTERSON,—When this shall fall into your hands, I shall have disappeared, under what circumstances I have not the penetration to foresee; but my instinct and all the circumstances of my nameless situation tell me that the end is sure and must be early. Go then, and first read the narrative which Lanyon warned me he was to place in your hands; and if you care to hear more, turn to the confession of

"Your unworthy and unhappy friend,
"HENRY JEKYLL."

"There was a third inclosure?" asked Utterson.

"Here, sir," said Poole, and gave into his hands a considerable packet sealed in several places.

The lawyer put it in his pocket. "I would say nothing of this paper. If your master has fled or is dead, we may at least save his credit. It is now ten; I must go home and read these documents in quiet; but I shall be back before midnight, when we shall send for the police."

They went out, locking the door of the theater behind them; and Utterson, once more leaving the servants gathered about the fire in the hall, trudged back to his office to read the two narratives in which this mystery was now to be explained.

DOCTOR LANYON'S NARRATIVE

ON the ninth of January, now four days ago, I received by the evening delivery a registered envelope, addressed in the hand of my colleague and old school-companion, Henry Jekyll. I was a good deal surprised by this; for we were by no means in the habit of correspondence; I had seen the man, dined with him, indeed, the night before; and I could imagine nothing in our intercourse that should testify formality of registration. The contents increased my wonder; for this is how the letter ran:

"10th December, 18—.

"DEAR LANYON,—You are one of my oldest friends; and although we may have differed at times on scientific questions, I cannot remember, at least on my side, any break in our affection. There was never a day when, if you had said to me, 'Jekyll, my life, my honor, my reason depend upon you,' I would not have sacrificed my left hand to help you. Lanyon, my life, my honor, my reason, are all at your mercy; if you fail me to-night I am lost. You might suppose, after this preface, that I am going to ask you for something dishonorable to grant. Judge for yourself.

"I want you to postpone all other engagements for to-night—ay, even if you were summoned to the bedside of an emperor; to take a cab, unless your carriage should be actually at the door; and with this letter in your hand for consultation, to drive straight to my house. Poole, my butler, has his orders; you will find him waiting your arrival with a locksmith. The door of my cabinet is then to be forced; and you are to go in alone; to open the glazed press (letter E) on the left hand, breaking the lock if it be shut; and to draw out, *with all its contents as they stand,* the fourth drawer from the top or (which is the same thing) the third from the bottom. In my extreme distress of mind, I have a morbid fear of misdirecting you; but even if I am in error, you may know the right drawer by its contents; some powders, a vial, and a paper book. This drawer I beg of you to carry back with you to Cavendish Square exactly as it stands.

"That is the first part of the service; now for the second. You should be back, if you set out at once, on the receipt of this, long before midnight; but I will leave you that amount of margin, not only in the fear of one of those obstacles that can neither be prevented nor foreseen, but because an hour when your servants are in bed is to be preferred for what will then remain to do. At midnight, then, I have to ask you to be alone in your consulting-room, to admit with your own hand into the house a man who will present himself in my name, and to place in his hands the drawer that you will have brought with you from my cabinet. Then you will have played your part and earned my gratitude completely. Five minutes afterward, if you insist upon an explanation, you will have understood that these arrangements are of capital importance, and that by the neglect of one of them, fantastic as they must appear, you might have charged your conscience with my death or the shipwreck of my reason.

"Confident as I am that you will not trifle with this appeal, my heart sinks and my hand trembles at the bare thought of such a possibility. Think of me at this hour, in a strange place, laboring under a blackness of distress that no fancy can exaggerate, and yet well aware that, if you will but punctually serve me, my troubles will roll away like a story that is told. Serve me, my dear Lanyon, and save

"Your friend,

"H. J.

"P. S.—I had already sealed this up when a fresh terror struck upon my soul. It is possible that the postoffice may fail me, and this letter not come into your hands until to-morrow morning. In that case, dear Lanyon, do my errand when it shall be most convenient for you in the course of the day; and once more expect my messenger at midnight. It may then already be too late; and if that night passes without event, you will know that you have seen the last of Henry Jekyll."

Upon the reading of this letter I made sure my colleague was insane; but till that was proved beyond the possibility of doubt I felt bound to do as he requested. The less I understood of this farrago, the less I was in a position to judge of its importance; and an appeal so worded could not be set aside without a grave responsibility. I rose accordingly from table, got into a hansom, and drove straight to Jekyll's house. The butler was awaiting my arrival; he had received by the same post as mine a registered letter of instruction, and had sent at once for a locksmith and a carpenter. The tradesmen came while we were yet speaking; and we moved in a body to old Dr. Denman's surgical theater (from which, as you are doubtless aware) Jekyll's private cabinet is most conveniently entered. The door was very strong, the lock excellent; the carpenter avowed he would have great trouble, and have to do much damage, if force were to be used, and the locksmith was near despair. But this last was a handy fellow, and after two hours' work the door stood open. The press marked E was unlocked; and I took out the drawer, had it filled up with straw and tied in a sheet, and returned with it to Cavendish Square.

Here I proceeded to examine its contents. The powders were neatly enough made up, but not with the nicety of the dispensing chemist; so that it was plain they were of Jekyll's private manufacture; and when I opened one of the wrappers, I found what seemed to me a simple, crystalline salt of a white color. The vial, to which I next turned my attention, might have been about half ull of a blood-red liquor, which was highly pungent to the sense of smell, and seemed to me to contain phosphorous and some volatile ether. At the other ingredients, I could make no guess. The book was an ordinary version book, and contained little but a series of dates. These covered a period of many years, but I observed that the entries ceased nearly a year ago and quite abruptly. Here and there a brief remark was appended to a date, usually no more than a single word: "double" occurring perhaps six times in a total of several hundred entries; and once, very early in the list and followed by several marks of exclamation, "total failure!!!" All this, though it whetted my curiosity, told me little that was definite. Here were a vial of some tincture, a paper of some salt, and the record of a series of experiments that had led (like too many or Jekyll's investigations) to no end of practical usefulness.

How could the presence of these articles in my house

affect either the honor, the sanity, or the life of my flighty colleague? If his messenger could go to one place, why could he not go to another? And even granting some impediment, why was this gentleman to be received by me in secret? The more I reflected, the more convinced I grew that I was dealing with a case of cerebral disease; and though I dismissed my servants to bed, I loaded an old revolver that I might be found in some posture of self-defense.

Twelve o'clock had scarce rung out over London, ere the knocker sounded very gently on the door. I went myself at the summons, and found a small man crouching against the pillars of the portico.

"Are you come from Dr. Jekyll?" I asked.

He told me "yes" by a constrained gesture; and when I had bidden him enter, he did not obey me without a searching backward glance into the darkness of the square. There was a policeman not far off, advancing with his bull's-eye open; and at the sight, I thought my visitor started and made greater haste.

These particulars struck me, I confess, disagreeably; and as I followed him into the bright light of the consulting-room, I kept my hand ready on my weapon. Here, at last, I had a chance of clearly seeing him. I have never set eyes on him before, so much was certain. He was small, as I have said; I was struck besides with the shocking expression of his face, with his remarkable combination of great muscular activity and great apparent debility of constitution, and—last but not least—with the odd, subjective disturbance caused by his neighborhood. This bore some resemblance to incipient rigor, and was accompanied by a marked sinking of the pulse. At the time, I set it down to some idiosyncratic, personal distaste, and merely wondered at the acuteness of the symptoms; but I have since had reason to believe the cause to lie much deeper in the nature of man, and to turn on some nobler hinge than the principle of hatred.

This person (who had thus, from the first moment of his entrance, struck in me what I can only describe as a disgustful curiosity) was dressed in a fashion that would have made an ordinary person laughable; his clothes, that is to say, although they were of rich and sober fabric, were enormously too large for him in every measurement—the trousers hanging on his legs and rolled up to keep them from the ground, the waist of the coat below his haunches, and the collar sprawling wide upon his shoulders. Strange to relate, this ludicrous accouterment was far from moving me to laughter. Rather, as there was something abnormal and misbegotten in the very essence of the creature that now faced me—something seizing, surprising, and revolting—this fresh disparity seemed but to fit in with and to re-enforce it; so that to my interest in the man's nature and character, there was added a curiosity as to his origin, his life, his fortune, and status in the world.

These observations, though they have taken so great a space to be set down in, were yet the work of a few seconds. My visitor was, indeed, on fire with somber excitement.

"Have you got it?" he cried. "Have you got it?" And so lively was his impatience that he even laid his hand upon my arm and sought to shake me.

I put him back, conscious at his touch of a certain icy pang along my blood. "Come, sir," said I. "You forget that I have not yet the pleasure of your acquaintance.

Be seated, if you please.' And I showed him an example, and sat down myself in my customary seat and with as fair an imitation of my ordinary manner to a patient, as the lateness of the hour, the nature of my preoccupations, and the horror I had of my visitor, would suffer me to muster.

"I beg your pardon, Dr. Lanyon," he replied, civilly enough. "What you say is very well founded, and my impatience has shown its heels to my politeness. I come here at the instance of your colleague, Dr. Henry Jekyll, on a piece of business of some moment; and I understood——" he paused and put his hand to his throat, and I could see, in spite of his collected manner, that he was wrestling against the approaches of hysteria—"I understood a drawer——"

But here I took pity on my visitor's suspense, and some perhaps on my own growing curiosity.

"There it is, sir," said I, pointing to the drawer, where it lay on the floor behind a table and still covered with the sheet.

He sprung to it, and then paused, and laid his hand upon his heart; I could hear his teeth grate with the convulsive action of his jaws; and his face was so ghastly to see that I grew alarmed both for his life and reason.

"Compose yourself," said I.

He turned a dreadful smile to me, and as if with the decision of despair, plucked away at the sheet. At sight of the contents he uttered one loud sob of such immense relief that I sat petrified. And the next moment, in a voice that was already fairly well under control, "Have you a graduated glass?" he asked.

I rose from my place with something of an effort, and gave him what he asked.

He thanked me with a smiling nod, measured out a few minims of the red tincture and added one of the powders. The mixture, which was at first of a reddish hue, began, in proportion as the crystals melted, to brighten in color, to effervesce audibly, and to throw off small fumes of vapor. Suddenly and at the same moment the ebullition ceased and the compound changed to a dark purple, which faded again more slowly to a watery green. My visitor, who had watched these metamorphoses with a keen eye smiled, set down the glass upon the table, and then turned and looked upon me with an air of scrutiny.

"And now," said he, "to settle what remains. Will you be wise? will you be guided? will you suffer me to take this glass in my hand and to go forth from your house without further parley? or has the greed of curiosity too much command of you? Think before you answer, for it shall be done as you decide. As you decide, you shall be left as you were before, and neither richer nor wiser, unless the sense of service rendered to a man in mortal distress may be counted as a kind of riches of the soul. Or, if you shall so prefer to choose, a new province of knowledge and new avenues to fame and power shall be laid open to you, here, in this room, upon the instant; and your sight shall be blasted by a prodigy to stagger the unbelief of Satan."

"Sir," said I, affecting a coolness that I was far from truly possessing, "you speak enigmas, and you will, perhaps, not wonder that I hear you with no very strong impression of belief. But I have gone too far in the way of inexplicable services to pause before I see the end."

"It is well," replied my visitor. "Lanyon, you remember your vows: what follows is under the seal of our profession. And now, you who have so long been bound to the most narrow and material views, you who have denied the virtue of transcendental medicine, you who have derided your superiors—behold!"

He put the glass to his lips, and drank at one gulp. A cry followed; he reeled, staggered, clutched at the table, and held on, staring with injected eyes, gasping with open mouth; and, as I looked, there came, I thought, a change; he seemed to swell; his face became suddenly black, and the features seemed to melt and alter—and the next moment I had sprung to my feet and leaped back against the wall, my arm raised to shield me from that prodigy, my mind submerged in terror.

"O God!" I screamed, and "O God!" again and again; for there before my eyes—pale and shaking, and half fainting, and groping before him with his hands, like a man restored from death—there stood Henry Jekyll!

What he told me in the next hour I cannot bring my mind to set on paper. I saw what I saw, I heard what I heard, and my soul sickened at it; and yet now, when that sight has faded from my eyes, I ask myself if I believe it, and I cannot answer. My life is shaken to its roots; sleep has left me; the deadliest terror sits by me at all hours of the day and night; I feel that my days are numbered, and that I must die; and yet I shall die incredulous. As for the moral turpitude that man unveiled to me, even with tears of penitence, I cannot, even in memory, dwell on it without a start of horror. I will say but one thing, Utterson, and that (if you can bring your mind to credit it) will be more than enough. The creature who crept into my house that night was, on Jekyll's own confession, known by the name of Hyde, and hunted for in every corner of the land as the murderer of Carew.   HASTIE LANYON.

HENRY JEKYLL'S FULL STATEMENT OF THE CASE

I WAS born in the year 18— to a large fortune, endowed besides with excellent parts, inclined by nature to industry, fond of the respect of the wise and good among my fellowmen, and thus, as might have been supposed, with every guarantee of an honorable and distinguished future. And indeed the worst of my faults was a certain impatient gayety of disposition, such as has made the happiness of many, but such as I found it hard to reconcile with my imperious desire to carry my head high, and wear a more than commonly grave countenance before the public. Hence it came about that I concealed my pleasures; and that when I reached years of reflection, and began to look round me and take stock of my progress and position in the world, I stood already committed to a profound duplicity of life. Many a man would have even blazoned such irregularities as I was guilty of; but from the high views that I had set before me, I regarded and hid them with an almost morbid sense of shame. It was thus rather the exacting nature of my aspirations than any particular degradation in my faults, that made me what I was, and, with even a deeper trench than in the majority of men, severed in me those provinces of good and ill which divide and compound man's dual nature. In this case, I was driven to reflect deeply and inveterately on that hard law of life, which lies at the root of religion and is one of the most plentiful springs of distress.

Though so profound a double-dealer, I was in no sense a hypocrite; both sides of me were in dead earnest; I was no more myself when I laid aside restraint and plunged in shame, than when I labored, in the eye of day, at the furtherance of knowledge or the relief of sorrow and suffering. And it chanced that the direction of my scientific studies, which led wholly toward the mystic and the transcendental, reacted and shed a strong light on this consciousness of the perennial war among my members. With every day, and from both sides of my intelligence, the moral and the intellectual, I thus drew steadily nearer to that truth, by whose partial discovery I have been doomed to such a dreadful shipwreck; that man is not truly one, but truly two. I say two, because the state of my own knowledge does not pass beyond that point. Others will follow, others will outstrip me on the same lines; and I hazard the guess that man will be ultimately known for a mere polity of multifarious, incongruous, and independent denizens.

I, for my part, from the nature of my life, advanced infallibly in one direction, and in one direction only. It was on the moral side, and in my own person, that I learned to recognize the thorough and primitive duality of man; I saw that, of the two natures that contended in the field of my consciousness, even if I could rightly be said to be either, it was only because I was radically both; and from an early date, even before the course of my scientific discoveries had begun to suggest the most naked possibility of such a miracle, I had learned to dwell with

pleasure, as a beloved day-dream, on the thought of the
separation of these elements. If each, I told myself, could
but be housed in separate identities, life would be relieved
of all that was unbearable; the unjust might go his way,
delivered from the aspirations and remorse of his more
upright twin; and the just could walk steadfastly and securely on his upward path, doing the good things in which
he found his pleasure, and no longer exposed to disgrace
and penitence by the hands of this extraneous evil. It was
the curse of mankind that these incongruous fagots were
thus bound together—that in the agonized womb of consciousness, these polar twins should be continuously struggling. How, then, were they dissociated?

I was so far in my reflections when, as I have said, a
side light began to shine upon the subject from the laboratory table. I began to perceive more deeply than it has
ever yet been stated, the trembling immateriality, the
mistlike transcience, of this seemingly so solid body in
which we walk attired. Certain agents I found to have
the power to shake and to pluck back that fleshy vestment,
even as a wind might toss the curtains of a pavilion. For
two good reasons, I will not enter deeply into this scientific branch of my confession. First, because I have been
made to learn that the doom and burden of our life is
bound forever on man's shoulders, and when the attempt
is made to cast it off, it but returns upon us with more un-
familiar and more awful pressure. Second, because, as my
narrative will make, alas! too evident, my discoveries were
incomplete. Enough, then, that I not only recognized my
natural body for the mere aura and effulgence of certain
of the powers that made up my spirit, but managed to
compound a drug by which these powers should be de-

throned from their supremacy, and a second form and
countenance substituted, none the less natural to me because they were the expression, and bore the stamp, of
lower elements in my soul.

I hesitated long before I put this theory to the test of
practice. I knew well that I risked death; for any drug
that so potently controlled and shook the very fortress of
identity, might by the least scruple of an overdose or at
the least inopportunity in the moment of exhibition, utterly blot out that immaterial tabernacle which I looked
to it to change. But the temptation of a discovery so
singular and profound at last overcame the suggestions of
alarm. I had long since prepared my tincture; I purchased at once, from a firm of wholesale chemists, a large
quantity of a particular salt which I knew, from my experiments, to be the last ingredient required; and late one
accursed night, I compounded the elements, watched them
boil and smoke together in the glass, and when the ebullition had subsided, with a strong glow of courage, drank
off the potion.

The most racking pangs succeeded; a grinding in the
bones, deadly nausea, and a horror of the spirit that can
not be exceeded at the hour of birth or death. Then these
agonies began swiftly to subside, and I came to myself as
if out of a great sickness. There was something strange
in my sensations, something indescribably new and, from
its very novelty, incredibly sweet. I felt younger, lighter,
happier in body; within I was conscious of a heady reck-
lessness, a current of disordered sensual images running
like a mill race in my fancy, a dissolution of the bonds of
obligation, an unknown but not an innocent freedom of
the soul. I knew myself, at the first breath of this new

life, to be more wicked, tenfold more wicked, sold a slave to my original evil; and the thought, in that moment, braced and delighted me like wine. I stretched out my hands, exulting in the freshness of these sensations; and in the act, I was suddenly aware that I had lost in stature.

There was no mirror, at that date, in my room; that which stands beside me as I write, was brought there later on and for the very purpose of these transformations. The night, however, was far gone into the morning—the morning, black as it was, was nearly ripe for the conception of the day—the inmates of my house were locked in the most rigorous hours of slumber; and I determined, flushed as I was with hope and triumph, to venture in my new shape as far as to my bedroom. I crossed the yard, wherein the constellations looked down upon me, I could have thought, with wonder, the first creature of that sort that their unsleeping vigilance had yet disclosed to them; I stole through the corridors, a stranger in my own house; and coming to my room, I saw for the first time the appearance of Edward Hyde.

I must here speak by theory alone, saying not that which I know, but that which I suppose to be most probable. The evil side of my nature, to which I had now transferred the stamping efficacy, was less robust and less developed than the good which I had just deposed. Again, in the course of my life, which had been, after all, nine-tenths a life of effort, virtue, and control, it had been much less exercised and much less exhausted.

And hence, as I think, it came about that Edward Hyde was so much smaller, slighter, and younger than Henry Jekyll. Even as good shone upon the countenance of the one, evil was written broadly and plainly on the face of the other. Evil besides (which I must still believe to be the lethal side of man) had left on that body an imprint of deformity and decay. And yet when I looked upon that ugly idol in the glass, I was conscious of no repugnance, rather of a leap of welcome. This, too, was myself. It seemed natural and human. In my eyes it bore a livelier image of the spirit, it seemed more express and single, than the imperfect and divine countenance I had been hitherto accustomed to call mine. And in so far I was doubtless right. I have observed that when I wore the semblance of Edward Hyde, none could come near to me at first without a visible misgiving of the flesh. This, as I take it, was because all human beings, as we meet them, commingled out of good and evil; and Edward Hyde, alone in the ranks of mankind, was pure evil.

I lingered but a moment at the mirror; the second and conclusive experiment had yet to be attempted; it yet remained to be seen if I had lost my identity beyond redemption and must flee before daylight from a house that was no longer mine; and hurrying back to my cabinet, I once more prepared and drank the cup, once more suffered the pangs of dissolution, and came to myself once more with the character, the stature, and the face of Henry Jekyll.

That night I had come to the fatal cross-roads. Had I approached my discovery in a more noble spirit, had I risked the experiment while under the empire of generous or pious aspirations, all must have been otherwise, and from these agonies of death and birth I had come forth an angel instead of a fiend. The drug had no discriminating action; it was neither diabolical nor divine; it but shook the doors of the prison-house of my disposition; and like the captives of Philippi, that which stood within ran forth. At that time my virtue slumbered; my evil, kept awake by ambition, was alert and swift to seize the occasion; and the thing that was projected was Edward Hyde. Hence, although I had now two characters as well as two appearances, one was wholly evil, and the other was still the old Henry Jekyll, that incongruous compound of whose reformation and improvement I had already learned to despair. The movement was thus wholly toward the worse.

Even at that time, I had not yet conquered my aversion to the dryness of a life of study. I would still be merrily disposed at times; and as my pleasures were (to say the least) undignified, and I was not only well known and highly considered, but growing toward the elderly man, this incoherency of my life was daily growing more unwelcome. It was on this side that my new power tempted me until I fell in slavery. I had but to drink the cup to doff at once the body of the noted professor, and to assume, like a thick cloak, that of Edward Hyde. I smiled at the notion; it seemed to me at the time to be humorous; and I made my preparations with the most studious care. I took and furnished that house in Soho, to which Hyde was tracked by the police; and engaged as a housekeeper a creature whom I well knew to be silent and unscrupulous. On the other side, I announced to my servants that a Mr. Hyde (whom I described) was to have full liberty and power about my house in the Square; and to parry mishaps, I even called and made myself a familiar object, in my second character. I next drew up that will to which you so much objected; so that if anything befell me in the person of Dr. Jekyll I could enter on that of Edward Hyde without pecuniary loss. And thus fortified, as I supposed, on every side, I began to profit by the strange immunities of my position.

Men have before hired bravoes to transact their crimes, while their own person and reputation sat under shelter. I was the first that ever did so for his pleasures. I was the first that could thus plod in the public eye with a load of genial respectability, and in a moment, like a schoolboy, strip off these lendings and spring headlong into the sea of liberty. But for me, in my impenetrable mantle, the safety was complete. Think of it—I did not even exist! Let me but escape into my laboratory door, give me but a second or two to mix and swallow the draught that I had always standing ready; and whatever he had done, Edward Hyde would pass away like the stain of breath upon a mirror; and there in his stead, quietly at home, trimming the midnight lamp in his study, a man who could afford to laugh at suspicion, would be Henry Jekyll.

The pleasures which I made haste to seek in my disguise were, as I have said, undignified; I would scarce use a harder term. But in the hands of Edward Hyde, they soon began to turn toward the monstrous. When I would come back from these excursions, I was often plunged into a kind of wonder at my vicarious depravity. This familiar that I called out of my own soul, and sent forth to do his good pleasure, was a being inherently malign and villainous; his every act and thought centered on self; drinking pleasure with bestial avidity from one degree of torture to another; relentless like a man of stone. Henry Jekyll stood at times aghast before the acts of Edward Hyde; but the situation was apart from ordinary laws, and insidiously relaxed the grasp of conscience. It was Hyde, after all,

and Hyde alone, that was guilty. Jekyll was no worse; he
woke again to his good qualities seemingly unimpaired;
he would even make haste, where it was possible, to undo
the evil done by Hyde. And thus his conscience slumbered.

Into the details of the infamy at which I thus connived
(for even now I can scarce grant that I committed it) I
have no design of entering; I mean but to point out the
warnings and the successive steps with which my chastise-
ment approached. I met with one accident which, as it
brought on no consequence, I shall no more than mention. An act of cruelty to a child aroused against me the
anger of a passerby, whom I recognized the other day in
the person of your kinsman; the doctor and the child's
family joined him; there were moments when I feared for
my life; and, at last, in order to pacify their too just re-
sentment, Edward Hyde had to bring them to the door,
and pay them in a check drawn in the name of Henry
Jekyll. But this danger was easily eliminated from the future, by opening an account at another bank in the name
of Edward Hyde himself; and when, by sloping my own
hand backward, I had supplied my double with a signature, I thought I sat beyond the reach of fate.

Some two months before the murder of Sir Danvers, I
had been out for one of my adventures, had returned at a
late hour, and woke the next day in bed with somewhat odd
sensations. It was in vain I looked about me; in vain I saw
the decent furniture and tall proportions of my room in the
square; in vain that I recognized the pattern of the bed curtains and the design of the mahogany frame; something
still kept insisting that I was not where I was, that I had not
wakened where I seemed to be, but in the little room in

Soho where I was accustomed to sleep in the body of Edward Hyde. I smiled to myself, and, in my psychological way, began lazily to inquire into the elements of this illusion, occasionally, even as I did so, dropping back into a comfortable morning doze. I was still so engaged when, in one of my more wakeful moments, my eyes fell upon my hand. Now the hand of Henry Jekyll (as you have often remarked) was professional in shape and size; it was large, firm, white, and comely. But the hand which I now saw, clearly enough, in the yellow light of a mid-London morning, lying half shut on the bedclothes, was lean, corded, knuckly, of a dusky pallor and thickly shaded with a swart growth of hair. It was the hand of Edward Hyde.

I must have stared upon it for near half a minute, sunk as I was in the mere stupidity of wonder, before terror woke up in my breast as sudden and startling as the crash of cymbals; and bounding from my bed, I rushed to the mirror. At the sight that met my eyes, my blood was changed into something exquisitely thin and icy. Yes, I had gone to bed Henry Jekyll, I had awakened Edward Hyde. How was this to be explained? I asked myself; and then, with another bound of terror—how was it to be remedied? It was well on in the morning; the servants were up; all my drugs were in the cabinet—a long journey down two pairs of stairs, through the back passage, across the open court and through the anatomical theater, from where I was then standing horror-struck. It might indeed be possible to cover my face; but of what use was that, when I was unable to conceal the alteration in my stature? And then with an overpowering sweetness of relief it came back upon my mind that the servants were already used to the coming and going of my second self. I had soon dressed, as well as I was able, in clothes of my own size; had soon passed through the house, where Bradshaw stared and drew back at seeing Mr. Hyde at such an hour and in such a strange array; and ten minutes later Dr. Jekyll had returned to his own shape and was sitting with a darkened brow, to make a feint of breakfasting.

Small indeed was my appetite. This inexplicable incident, this reversal of my previous experience, seemed, like the Babylonian finger on the wall, to be spelling out the letters of my judgment; and I began to reflect more seriously than ever before on the issues and possibilities of my double existence. That part of me which I had the power of projecting, had lately been much exercised and nourished; it had seemed to me of late as though the body of Edward Hyde had grown in stature, as though (when I wore that form) I were conscious of a more generous tide of blood; and I began to spy a danger that, if this were much prolonged, the balance of my nature might be permanently overthrown, the power of voluntary change be forfeited, and the character of Edward Hyde become irrevocably mine. The power of the drug had not been always equally displayed. Once, very early in my career, it had totally failed me; since then I had been obliged on more than one occasion to double, and once, with infinite risk of death, to treble the amount; and those rare uncertainties had cast hitherto the sole shadow on my contentment. Now, however, and in the light of that morning's accident, I was led to remark that whereas, in the beginning, the difficulty had been to throw off the body of Jekyll, it had of late, gradually but decidedly, transferred itself to the other side. All things therefore seemed to point to this: that I was slowly losing hold of my original and better self, and becoming slowly incorporated with my second and worse.

Between these two, I now felt I had to choose. My two natures had memory in common, but all other faculties were most unequally shared between them. Jekyll (who was composite) now with the most sensitive apprehensions, now with a greedy gusto, projected and shared in the pleasures and adventures of Hyde; but Hyde was indifferent to Jekyll, or but remembered him as the mountain bandit remembers the cavern in which he conceals himself from pursuit. Jekyll had more than a father's interest; Hyde had more than a son's indifference. To cast in my lot with Jekyll, was to die to those appetites which I had long secretly indulged and had of late begun to pamper. To cast it in with Hyde was to die to a thousand interests and aspirations, and to become, at a blow and forever, despised and friendless. The bargain might appear unequal; but there was still another consideration in the scales; for while Jekyll would suffer smartingly in the fires of abstinence, Hyde would not be even conscious of all that he had lost. Strange as my circumstances were, the terms of this debate are as old and commonplace as man; much the same inducements and alarms cast the die for any tempted and trembling sinner; and it fell out with me, as it falls with so vast a majority of my fellows, that I chose the better part and was found wanting in the strength to keep to it.

Yes, I preferred the elderly and discontented doctor, surrounded by friends and cherishing honest hopes; and bade a resolute farewell to the liberty, the comparative youth, the light step, leaping impulses and secret pleasures, that I had enjoyed in the disguise of Hyde. I made this choice perhaps with some unconscious reservation, for I neither gave up the house in Soho, nor destroyed the clothes of Edward Hyde, which still lay ready in my cabinet. For two months, however, I was true to my determination; for two months, I led a life of such severity as I had never before attained to, and enjoyed the compensation of an approving conscience. But time began at last to obliterate the freshness of my alarm; the praises of conscience began to grow into a thing of course; I began to be tortured with throes and longings, as of Hyde struggling after freedom; and at last, in an hour of moral weakness, I once again compounded and swallowed the transforming draught.

I do not suppose that, when a drunkard reasons with himself upon his vice, he is once out of five hundred times affected by the dangers that he runs through his brutish, physical insensibility; neither had I, long as I had considered my position, made enough allowance for the complete moral insensibility and insensate readiness to evil, which were the leading characters of Edward Hyde. Yet it was by these that I was punished. My devil had been long caged, he came out roaring. I was conscious, even when I took the draught, of a more unbridled, a more furious propensity to ill. It must have been this, I suppose, that stirred in my soul that tempest of impatience with which I listened to the civilities of my unhappy victim; I declare, at least, before God, no man morally sane could have been guilty of that crime upon so pitiful a provocation; and that I struck in no more reasonable spirit than that in which a sick child may break a plaything. But I had voluntarily stripped myself of all those balancing instincts, by which even the worst of us continues to walk with some degree of steadiness among temptations; and in my case, to be tempted, however slightly, was to fall.

Instantly the spirit of hell awoke in me and raged. With a transport of glee I mauled the unresisting body, tasting delight from every blow; and it was not till weariness had begun to succeed, that I was suddenly, in the top fit of my delirium, struck through the heart by a cold thrill of terror. A mist dispersed; I saw my life to be forfeit, and fled from the scene of these excesses, at once glorying and trembling, my lust of evil gratified and stimulated, my love of life screwed to the topmost peg. I ran to the house in Soho and (to make assurance doubly sure) destroyed my papers; thence I set out through the lamplit streets, in the same divided ecstasy of mind, gloating on my crime, light-headedly devising others in the future, and yet still hastening and still hearkening in my wake for the steps of the avenger. Hyde had a song upon his lips as he compounded the draught, and as he drank it, pledged the dead man. The pangs of transformation had not done tearing him, before Henry Jekyll, with streaming tears of gratitude and remorse, had fallen upon his knees and lifted his clasped hands to God. The veil of self-indulgence was rent from head to foot, I saw my life as a whole; I followed it up from the days of childhood, when I had walked with my father's hand, and through the self-denying toils of my professional life, to arrive again and again, with the same sense of unreality, at the damned horrors of the evening.

I could have screamed aloud; I sought with tears and prayers to smother down the crowd of hideous images and sounds with which my memory swarmed against me; and still, between the petitions, the ugly face of my iniquity

stared into my soul. As the acuteness of this remorse began to die away, it was succeeded by a sense of joy. The
problem of my conduct was solved. Hyde was thenceforth
impossible; whether I would or not, I was now confined to
the better part of my existence; and oh, how I rejoiced to
think it! with what willing humility I embraced anew the
restrictions of natural life! with what sincere renunciation
I locked the door by which I had so often gone and come,
and ground the key under my heel!

The next day came the news that the murder had been
discovered, that the guilt of Hyde was patent to the world,
and that the victim was a man high in public estimation.
It was not only a crime, it had been a tragic folly. I think
I was glad to know it; I think I was glad to have my better
impulses thus buttressed and guarded by the terrors of the
scaffold. Jekyll was now my city of refuge; let but Hyde
peep out an instant, and the hands of all men would be
raised to take and slay him.

I resolved in my future conduct to redeem the past; and
I can say with honesty that my resolve was fruitful of some
good. You know yourself how earnestly in the last months
of last year I labored to relieve suffering; you know that
much was done for others, and that the days passed quietly, almost happily, for myself. Nor can I truly say that I
wearied of this beneficent and innocent life; I think instead that I daily enjoyed it more completely; but I was
still cursed with my duality of purpose; and as the first
edge of my penitence wore off, the lower side of me, so
long indulged, so recently chained down, began to growl
for license. Not that I dreamed of resuscitating Hyde, the
bare idea of that would startle me to frenzy; no, it was in
my own person, that I was once more tempted to trifle

with my conscience; and it was as an ordinary secret sinner, that I at last fell before the assaults of temptation.

There comes an end to all things; the most capacious measure is filled at last; and this brief condescension to my evil finally destroyed the balance of my soul. And yet I was not alarmed; the fall seemed natural, like a return to the old days before I had made my discovery. It was a fine, clear, January day, wet under foot where the frost had melted, but cloudless overhead; and the Regent's Park was full of winter chirrupings, and sweet with spring odors. I sat in the sun on a bench; the animal within me licking the chops of memory; the spiritual side a little drowsed, promising subsequent penitence, but not yet moved to begin. After all, I reflected, I was like my neighbors; and then I smiled, comparing myself with other men, comparing my active good-will with the lazy cruelty of their neglect. And at the very moment of that vainglorious thought, a qualm came over me, a horrid nausea and the most deadly shuddering. These passed away, and left me faint; and then, as in its turn the faintness subsided, I began to be aware of a change in the temper of my thoughts, a greater boldness, a contempt of danger, a solution of the bonds of obligation. I looked down; my clothes hung formlessly on my shrunken limbs; the hand that lay on my knee was corded and hairy. I was once more Edward Hyde. A moment before I had been safe of all men's respect, wealthy, beloved—the cloth laying for me in the dining-room at home; and now I was the common quarry of mankind, hunted, houseless, a known murderer, thrall to the gallows.

My reason wavered, but it did not fail me utterly. I have more than once observed that, in my second character, my faculties seemed sharpened to a point and my spirits more tensely elastic; thus it came about that where Jekyll perhaps might have succumbed, Hyde rose to the importance of the moment. My drugs were in one of the presses of my cabinet; how was I to reach them? That was the problem that (crushing my temples in my hands) I set myself to solve. The laboratory door I had closed. If I sought to enter by the house, my own servants would consign me to the gallows. I saw I must employ another hand, and thought of Lanyon. How was he to be reached? how persuaded? Supposing that I escaped capture in the streets, how was I to make my way into his presence? and how should I, an unknown and displeasing visitor, prevail on the famous physician to rifle the study of his colleague, Dr. Jekyll? Then I remembered that of my original character, one part remained to me; I could write my own hand; and once I had conceived that kindling spark, the way that I must follow became lighted up from end to end.

Thereupon, I arranged my clothes as best I could, and summoning a passing hansom, drove to an hotel in Portland Street, the name of which I chanced to remember. At my appearance (which was indeed comical enough, however tragic a fate these garments covered) the driver could not conceal his mirth. I gnashed my teeth upon him with a gust of devilish fury; and the smile withered from his face—happily for him—yet more happily for myself, for in another instant I had certainly dragged him from his perch. At the inn, as I entered, I looked about me with so black a countenance as made the attendants tremble; not a look did they exchange in my presence; but obsequiously took my orders, led me to a private room,

and brought me wherewithal to write. Hyde, in danger of
his life, was a creature new to me; shaken with inordinate
anger, strung to the pitch of murder, lusting to inflict
pain. Yet the creature was astute; mastered his fury with
a great effort of the will; composed his two important letters, one to Lanyon and one to Poole; and that he might
receive actual evidence of their being posted, sent them
out with directions that they should be registered.

Thenceforward, he sat all day over the fire in the private room, gnawing his nails; there he dined, sitting alone
with his fears, the waiter visibly quailing before his eye;
and thence, when the night was fully come, he set forth in
the corner of a closed cab, and was driven to and fro about
the streets of the city. He, I say—I cannot say I. That
child of hell had nothing human; nothing lived in him
but fear and hatred. And when at last, thinking the driver had begun to grow suspicious, he discharged the cab
and ventured on foot, attired in his misfitting clothes, an
object marked out for observation, into the midst of the
nocturnal passengers, these tow base passions raged within
him like a tempest. He walked fast, hunted by his fears,
chattering to himself, skulking through the less frequent-
ed thoroughfares, counting the minutes that still divided
him from midnight. Once a woman spoke to him, offering, I think, a box of lights. He smote her in the face, and
she fled.

When I came to myself at Lanyon's, the horror of my
old friend perhaps affected me somewhat; I do not know;
it was least but a drop in the sea to the abhorrence with
which I looked back upon these hours. A change had
come over me. It was no longer the fear of the gallows,
it was the horror of being Hyde that racked me. I re-

ceived Lanyon's condemnation partly in a dream; it was partly in a dream that I came home to my own house and got into bed. I slept after the prostration of the day, with a stringent and profound slumber which not even the nightmares that wrung me could avail to break. I awoke in the morning shaken, weakened, but refreshed. I still hated and feared the thought of the brute that slept within me, and I had not of course forgotten the appalling dangers of the day before; but I was once more at home, in my own house, and close to my drugs; and gratitude for my escape shone so strong in my soul that it almost rivaled the brightness of hope.

I was stepping leisurely across the court after breakfast, drinking the chill of the air with pleasure, when I was seized again with those indescribable sensations that heralded the change; and I had but the time to gain the shelter of my cabinet, before I was once again raging and freezing with the passions of Hyde. It took on this occasion a double dose to recall me to myself; and alas! six hours after, as I sat looking sadly in the fire, the pangs returned, and the drug had to be readministered. In short, from that day forth it seemed only by a great effort as of gymnastics, and only under the immediate stimulation of the drug, that I was able to wear the countenance of Jekyll. At all hours of the day and night, I would be taken with the premonitory shudder; above all, if I slept, or even dozed for a moment in my chair, it was always as Hyde that I awakened. Under the strain of this continually impending doom and by the sleeplessness to which I now condemned myself, ay, even beyond what I had thought possible to man, I became, in my own person, a creature eaten up and emptied by fever, languidly weak both in body and mind, and solely occupied by one thought: the horror of my other self. But when I slept, or when the virtue of the medicine wore off, I would leap almost without transition (for the pangs of transformation grew daily less marked) into the possession of a fancy brimming with images of terror, a soul boiling with cause-less hatreds, and a body that seemed not strong enough to contain the raging energies of life.

The powers of Hyde seemed to have grown with the sickliness of Jekyll. And certainly the hate that now di-vided them was equal on each side. With Jekyll, it was a thing of vital instinct. He had now seen the full deform-ity of that creature that shared with him some of the phen-omena of consciousness, and was co-heir with him to death; and beyond these links of community, which in them-selves made the most poignant part of his distress, he thought of Hyde, for all his energy of life, as of something not only hellish but inorganic. This was the shocking thing; that the slime of the pit seemed to utter cries and voices; that the amorphous dust gesticulated and sinned; that what was dead and had no shape should usurp the offices of life. And this again, that this insurgent horror was knit to him closer than a wife, closer than an eye lay caged in his flesh, where he heard it mutter and felt it struggle to be born; and at every hour of weakness, and in the confidence of slumber, prevailed against him, and deposed him out of life.

The hatred of Hyde for Jekyll was of a different order. His terror of the gallows drove him continually to commit temporary suicide, and return to his subordinate station of a part instead of a person; but he loathed the necessity, he loathed the despondency into which Jekyll was now fallen, and he resented the dislike with which he was him-self regarded. Hence the ape-like tricks that he would play me, scrawling in my own hand blasphemies on the pages of my books, burning the letters and destroying the portrait of my father; and indeed, had it not been for his fear of death, he would long ago have ruined himself in order to involve me in the ruin. But his love of life is wonderful; I go further; I who sicken and freeze at the mere thought of him, when I recall the abjection and pas-sion of this attachment, and when I know how he fears my power to cut him off by suicide, I find it in my heart to pity him.

It is useless, and the time awfully fails me, to prolong this description; no one has ever suffered such torments, let that suffice; and yet even to these, habit brought—no, not alleviation—but a certain callousness of soul, a certain acquiescence of despair; and my punishment might have gone on for years, but for the last calamity which has now fallen, and which has finally severed me from my own face and nature. My provision of the salt, which had never been renewed since the date of the first experiment, began to run low. I sent out for a fresh supply, and mixed the draught; the ebullition followed, and the first change of color, not the second; I drank it, and it was without ef-ficacy. You will learn from Poole how I have had London ransacked; it was in vain; and I am now persuaded that my first supply was impure, and that it was that unknown impurity which lent efficacy to the draught.

About a week has passed, and I am now finishing this statement under the influence of the last of the old pow-ders. This, then, is the last time, short of a miracle, that Henry Jekyll can think his own thoughts, or see his own face (now how sadly altered!) in the glass. Nor must I delay too long to bring my writing to an end; for if my narrative has hitherto escaped destruction, it has been by a combination of great prudence and great good luck. Should the throes of change take me in the act of writing it, Hyde will tear it in pieces; but if some time shall have elapsed after I have laid it by, his wonderful selfishness and circumspection for the moment will probably save it once again from the action of his ape-like spite. And indeed the doom that is closing on us both, has already changed and crushed him. Half an hour from now, when I shall again and forever reindue that hated personality, I know how I shall sit shuddering and weeping in my chair, or continue, with the most strained and fear-struck ecstasy of listening, to pace up and down this room (my last earthly refuge), and give ear to every sound of menace. Will Hyde die upon the scaffold? or will he find courage to release himself at the last moment? God knows; I am careless; this is my true hour of death, and what is to follow concerns another than myself. Here then, as I lay down the pen and proceed to seal up my confession, I bring the life of that unhappy Henry Jekyll to an end.

THE END

TRAVELS WITH A DONKEY
IN THE CEVENNES

EDITORIAL NOTE

TRAVELS WITH A DONKEY IN THE CEVENNES was first published in June, 1879, and bore the imprint of C. Kegan Paul & Co. As with AN INLAND VOYAGE, it reached a second edition in 1881 at the hands of the same publishers. Later, the rights were purchased by Stevenson's father, who transferred the plates to Messrs. Chatto and Windus, who issued a new edition in 1884. The book was reprinted in America immediately upon its appearance in England, the first American edition bearing date of 1879.

It is a record of wanderings during the autumn (September and October) of 1878; the manuscript having been prepared during the winter of 1878-79.

MY DEAR SIDNEY COLVIN,

The journey which this little book is to describe was very agreeable and fortunate for me. After an uncouth beginning, I had the best of luck to the end. But we are all travellers in what John Bunyan calls the wilderness of this world,—all, too, travellers with a donkey; and the best that we find in our travels is an honest friend. He is a fortunate voyager who finds many. We travel, indeed, to find them. They are the end and the reward of life. They keep us worthy of ourselves; and when we are alone, we are only nearer to the absent.

Every book is, in an intimate sense, a circular letter to the friends of him who writes it. They alone take his meaning; they find private messages, assurances of love, and expressions of gratitude dropped for them in every corner. The public is but a generous patron who defrays the postage. Yet, though the letter is directed to all, we have an old and kindly custom of addressing it on the outside to one. Of what shall a man be proud, if he is not proud of his friends? And so, my dear Sidney Colvin, it is with pride that I sign myself affectionately yours,

R. L. S.

VELAY

"*Many are the mighty things, and nought is more mighty
than man.
He masters by his devices the tenant of the fields.*"
—ANTIGONE.
'*Who hath loosed the bands of the wild ass?*"—JOB.

VELAY

THE DONKEY, THE PACK, AND THE PACK-SADDLE

IN a little place called *Le Monastier*, in a pleasant highland valley fifteen miles from *Le Puy*, I spent about a month of fine days. *Monastier* is notable for the making of lace, for drunkenness, for freedom of language, and for unparalleled political dissension. There are adherents of each of the four French parties—Legitimists, Orleanists, Imperialists, and Republicans—in this little mountain-town; and they all hate, loathe, decry, and calumniate each other. Except for business purposes, or to give each other the lie in a tavern brawl, they have laid aside even the civility of speech. 'Tis a mere mountain *Poland*. In the midst of this *Babylon* I found myself a rallying-point; every one was anxious to be kind and helpful to the stranger. This was not merely from the natural hospitality of mountain people, nor even from the surprise with which I was regarded as a man living of his own free will in *Monastier*, when he might just as well have lived anywhere else in this big world; it arose a good deal from my projected excursion southward through the *Cevennes*. A traveller of my sort was a thing hitherto unheard of in that district. I was looked upon with contempt, like a man who should project a journey to the moon, but yet with a respectful interest, like one setting forth for the

inclement Pole. All were ready to help in my preparations; a crowd of sympathizers supported me at the critical
moment of a bargain; not a step was taken but was heralded by glasses round and celebrated by a dinner or a break·
fast.

It was already hard upon *October* before I was ready to
set forth, and at the high altitudes over which my road lay
there was no Indian summer to be looked for. I was determined, if not to camp out, at least to have the means
of camping out in my possession; for there is nothing more
harassing to an easy mind than the necessity of reaching
shelter by dusk, and the hospitality of a village inn is not
always to be reckoned sure by those who trudge on foot.
A tent, above all for a solitary traveller, is troublesome to
pitch, and troublesome to strike again; and even on the
march it forms a conspicuous feature in your baggage. A
sleeping-sack, on the other hand, is always ready—you
have only to get into it; it serves a double purpose—a bed
by night, a portmanteau by day; and it does not advertise
your intention of camping out to every curious passer-by.
This is a huge point. If the camp is not secret, it is but a
troubled resting-place; you become a public character;
the convivial rustic visits your bedside after an early supper; and you must sleep with one eye open, and be up
before the day. I decided on a sleeping-sack; and after repeated visits to *Le Puy,* and a deal of high living for myself and my advisers, a sleeping-sack was designed, con-
structed, and triumphally brought home.

This child of my invention was nearly six feet square,
exclusive of two triangular flaps to serve as a pillow by
night and as the top and bottom of the sack by day. I call
it "the sack," but it was never a sack by more than cour-

tesy: only a sort of long roll or sausage, green water-proof cart-cloth without and blue sheep's fur within. It was commodious as a valise, warm and dry for a bed. There was luxurious turning room for one; and at a pinch the thing might serve for two. I could bury myself in it up to the neck; for my head I trusted to a fur cap, with a hood to fold down over my ears and a band to pass under my nose like a respirator; and in case of heavy rain I proposed to make myself a little tent, or tentlet, with my water-proof coat, three stones, and a bent branch.

It will readily be conceived that I could not carry this huge package on my own, merely human, shoulders. It remained to choose a beast of burden. Now, a horse is a fine lady among animals, flighty, timid, delicate in eating, of tender health; he is too valuable and too restive to be left alone, so that you are chained to your brute as to a fellow galley-slave; a dangerous road puts him out of his wits; in short, he's an uncertain and exacting ally, and adds thirty-fold to the troubles of the voyager. What I required was something cheap and small and hardy, and of a stolid and peaceful temper; and all these requisites pointed to a donkey.

There dwelt an old man in *Monastier,* of rather unsound intelligent according to some, much followed by street-boys, and known to fame as *Father Adam. Father Adam* had a cart, and to draw the cart a diminutive she-ass, not much bigger than a dog, the color of a mouse, with a kindly eye and a determined under-jaw. There was something neat and high-bred, a quakerish elegance, about the rogue that hit my fancy on the spot. Our first interview was in *Monastier* market-place. To prove her good temper, one child after another was set upon her back to ride, and

one after another went head over heels into the air; until
a want of confidence began to reign in youthful bosoms,
and the experiment was discontinued from a dearth of
subjects. I was already backed by a deputation of my
friends; but as if this were not enough, all the buyers and
sellers came round and helped me in the bargain; and the
ass and I and *Father Adam* were the centre of a hubbub
for near half an hour. At length she passed into my service for the consideration of sixty-five francs and a glass of
brandy. The sack had already cost eighty francs and two
glasses of beer; so that *Modestine,* as I instantly baptized
her, was upon all accounts the cheaper article. Indeed, that
was as it should be; for she was only an appurtenance of my
mattress, or self-acting bedstead on four castors.

I had a last interview with *Father Adam* in a billiard-
room at the witching hour of dawn, when I administered
the brandy. He professed himself greatly touched by the
separation, and declared he had often bought white bread
for the donkey when he had been content with black bread
for himself; but this, according to the best authorities, must
have been a flight of fancy. He had a name in the village
for brutally misusing the ass; yet it is certain that he shed
a tear, and the tear made a clean mark down one cheek.

By the advice of a fallacious local saddler, a leather pad
was made for me with rings to fasten on my bundle; and I
thoughtfully completed my kit and arranged my toilette.
By way of armory and utensils, I took a revolver, a little
spirit-lamp and pan, a lantern and some halfpenny candles,
a jack-knife and a large leather flask. The main cargo con-
sisted of two entire changes of warm clothing—besides my
travelling wear of country velveteen, pilot-coat, and knitted
spencer—some books, and my railway-rug, which, being

also in the form of a bag, made me a double castle for cold nights. The permanent larder was represented by cakes of chocolate and tins of Bologna sausage. All this, except what I carried about my person, was easily stowed into the sheepskin bag; and by good fortune I threw in my empty knapsack, rather for convenience of carriage than from any thought that I should want it on my journey. For more immediate needs, I took a leg of cold mutton, a bottle of Beaujolais, an empty bottle to carry milk, an egg-beater, and a considerable quantity of black bread and white, like *Father Adam,* for myself and donkey, only in my scheme of things the destinations were reversed.

Monastrians, of all shades of thought in politics, had agreed in threatening me with many ludicrous misadventures, and with sudden death in many surprising forms. Cold, wolves, robbers, above all the nocturnal practical joker, were daily and eloquently forced on my attention. Yet in these vaticinations, the true, patent danger was left out. Like *Christian,* it was from my pack I suffered by the way. Before telling my own mishaps, let me, in two words, relate the lesson of my experience. If the pack is well strapped at the ends, and hung at full length—not doubled, for your life—across the pack-saddle, the traveller is safe. The saddle will certainly not fit, such is the imperfection of our transitory life; it will assuredly topple and tend to overset; but there are stones on every roadside, and a man soon learns the art of correcting any tendency to over-balance with a well-adjusted stone.

On the day of my departure I was up a little after five; by six, we began to load the donkey; and ten minutes after, my hopes were in the dust. The pad would not stay on *Modestine's* back for half a moment. I returned it to

its maker, with whom I had so contumelious a passage that
the street outside was crowded from wall to wall with
gossips looking on and listening. The pad changed hands
with much vivacity; perhaps it would be more descriptive
to say that we threw it at each other's heads; and, at any
rate, we were very warm and unfriendly, and spoke with
a deal of freedom.

I had a common donkey pack-saddle—a *barde*, as they
call it—fitted upon *Modestine;* and once more loaded her
with my effects. The doubled sack, my pilot-coat (for it
was warm, and I was to walk in my waistcoat), a great bar
of black bread, and an open basket containing the white
bread, the mutton, and the bottles, were all corded together in a very elaborate system of knots, and I looked
on the result with fatuous content. In such a monstrous
deck-cargo, all poised *above* the donkey's shoulders, with
nothing below to balance, on a brand-new pack-saddle
that had not yet been worn to fit the animal, and fastened
with brand-new girths that might be expected to stretch
and slacken by the way, even a very careless traveller
should have seen disaster brewing. That elaborate system
of knots, again, was the work of too many sympathizers to
be very artfully designed. It is true they tightened the
cords with a will; as many as three at a time would have a
foot against *Modestine's* quarters, and be hauling with
clenched teeth; but I learned afterwards that one thought-
ful person, without any exercise of force, can make a more
solid job than half a dozen heated and enthusiastic
grooms. I was then but a novice; even after the misadventure of the pad nothing could disturb my security, and
I went forth from the stable-door as an ox goeth to the
slaughter.

THE GREEN DONKEY-DRIVER

THE bell of *Monastier* was just striking nine as I got quit of these preliminary troubles and descended the hill through the common. As long as I was within sight of the windows, a secret shame and the fear of some laughable defeat withheld me from tampering with *Modestine.* She tripped along upon her four small hoofs with a sober daintiness of gait; from time to time she shook her ears or her tail; and she looked so small under the bundle that my mind misgave me. We got across the ford without difficulty—there was no doubt about the matter, she was docility itself and once on the other bank, where the road begins to mount through pine-woods, I took in my right hand the unhallowed staff, and with a quaking spirit applied it to the donkey. *Modestine* brisked up her pace for perhaps three steps, and then relapsed into her former minuet. Another application had the same effect, and so with the third. I am worthy the name of an Englishman, and it goes against my conscience to lay my hand rudely on a female. I desisted, and looked her all over from head to foot; the poor brute's knees were trembling and her breathing was distressed; it was plain that she could go no faster on a hill. God forbid, thought I, that I should brutalize this innocent creature; let her go at her own pace, and let me patiently follow.

What that pace was, there is no word mean enough to describe; it was something as much slower than a walk as a walk is slower than a run; it kept me hanging on each foot for an incredible length of time; in five minutes it exhausted the spirit and set up a fever in all the muscles of the leg. And yet I had to keep close at hand and measure my advance exactly upon hers; for if I dropped a few yards into the rear, or went on a few yards ahead, *Modestine* came instantly to a halt and began to browse. The thought that this was to last from here to *Alais* nearly broke my heart. Of all conceivable journeys, this promised to be the most tedious. I tried to tell myself it was a lovely day; I tried to charm my foreboding spirit with tobacco; but I had a vision ever present to me of the long, long roads, up hill and down dale, and a pair of figures ever infinitesimally moving, foot by foot, a yard to the minute, and, like things enchanted in a nightmare, approaching no nearer to the goal.

In the mean time there came up behind us a tall peasant, perhaps forty years of age, of an ironical snuffy countenance, and arrayed in the green tail-coat of the country. He overtook us hand over hand, and stopped to consider our pitiful advance.

"Your donkey," says he, "is very old?"

I told him, I believed not.

Then, he supposed, we had come far.

I told him, we had but newly left *Monastier*.

"*Et vous marchez comme ça!*" cried he; and, throwing back his head, he laughed long and heartily. I watched him, half prepared to feel offended, until he had satisfied his mirth; and then, "You must have no pity on these animals," said he; and, plucking a switch out of a thicket, he began to lace *Modestine* about the sternworks, uttering a cry. The rogue pricked up her ears and broke into a good round pace, which she kept up without flagging, and without exhibiting the least symptom of distress, as long as the peasant kept beside us. Her former panting and shaking had been, I regret to say, a piece of comedy.

My *deus ex machinâ,* before he left me, supplied some excellent, if inhumane, advice; presented me with the switch, which he declared she would feel more tenderly than my cane; and finally taught me the true cry or masonic word of donkey-driver, "Proot!" All the time, he regarded me with a comical incredulous air, which was embarrassing to confront; and smiled over my donkey-driving, as I might have smiled over his orthography, or his green tail-coat. But it was not my turn for the moment.

I was proud of my new lore, and thought I had learned the art to perfection. And certainly *Modestine* did wonders for the rest of the forenoon, and I had a breathing space to look about me. It was Sabbath; the mountain-fields were all vacant in the sunshine; and as we came down through *St. Martin de Frugères,* the church was crowded to the door, there were people kneeling without upon the steps, and the sound of the priest's chanting came forth out of the dim interior. It gave me a home feeling on the spot; for I am a countryman of the Sabbath, so to speak, and all Sabbath observances, like a Scotch accent, strike in me mixed feelings, grateful and the reverse. It is only a traveller, hurrying by like a person from another planet, who can rightly enjoy the peace and beauty of the great ascetic feast. The sight of the resting country does his spirit good. There is something better than music in the wide unusual silence; and it disposes him to amiable thoughts, like the sound of a little river or the warmth of sunlight.

In this pleasant humor I came down the hill to where *Goudet* stands in a green end of a valley, with *Château Beaufort* opposite upon a rocky steep, and the stream as clear as crystal, lying in a deep pool between them. Above and below, you may hear it wimpling over the stones, an amiable stripling of a river, which it seems absurd to call the *Loire*. On all sides, *Goudet* is shut in by mountains; rocky footpaths, practicable at best for donkeys, join it to the outer world of *France;* and the men and women drink and swear, in their green corner, or look up at the snow-clad peaks in winter from the threshold of their homes, in an isolation, you would think, like that of *Homer's* Cyclops. But it is not so; the postman reaches *Goudet* with the letter-bag; the aspiring youth of *Goudet* are within a day's walk of the railway at *Le Puy;* and here in the inn you may find an engraved portrait of the host's nephew, *Régis Senac,* "Professor of Fencing and Champion of the two *Americas,*" a distinction gained by him, along with the sum of five hundred dollars, at *Tammany Hall, New York,* on the 10th *April,* 1876.

I hurried over my midday meal, and was early forth again. But, alas, as we climbed the interminable hill upon the other side, 'Proot!' seemed to have lost its virtue. I prooted like a lion, I prooted mellifluously like a sucking-dove; but *Modestine* would be neither softened nor intimidated. She held doggedly to her pace; nothing but a blow would move her, and that only for a second. I must follow at her heels, incessantly belaboring. A moment's pause in this ignoble toil, and she relapsed into her own

private gait. I think I never heard of any one in as mean
a situation. I must reach the lake of *Bouchet*, where I
meant to camp, before sundown, and, to have even a hope
of this, I must instantly maltreat this uncomplaining animal. The sound of my own blows sickened me. Once,
when I looked at her, she had a faint resemblance to a
lady of my acquaintance who formerly loaded me with
kindness; and this increased my horror of my cruelty.

To make matters worse, we encountered another donkey, ranging at will upon the roadside; and this other
donkey chanced to be a gentleman. He and *Modestine*
met nickering for joy, and I had to separate the pair and
beat down their young romance with a renewed and feverish bastinado. If the other donkey had had the heart of a
male under his hide, he would have fallen upon me tooth
and hoof; and this was a kind of consolation—he was
plainly unworthy of *Modestine's* affection. But the incident saddened me, as did everything that spoke of my
donkey's sex.

It was blazing hot up the valley, windless, with vehe-
ment sun upon my shoulders; and I had to labor so con-
sistently with my stick that the sweat ran into my eyes.
Every five minutes, too, the pack, the basket, and the
pilot-coat would take an ugly slew to one side or the other;
and I had to stop *Modestine*, just when I had got her to
a tolerable pace of about two miles an hour, to tug, push,
shoulder, and readjust the load. And at last, in the village
of *Ussel*, saddle and all, the whole hypothec turned round
and grovelled in the dust below the donkey's belly. She,
none better pleased, incontinently drew up and seemed to
smile; and a party of one man, two women, and two chil-

dren came up, and, standing round me in a half-circle, encouraged her by their example.

I had the devil's own trouble to get the thing righted; and the instant I had done so, without hesitation, it toppled and fell down upon the other side. Judge if I was hot! And yet not a hand was offered to assist me. The man, indeed, told me I ought to have a package of a different shape. I suggested, if he knew nothing better to the point in my predicament, he might hold his tongue. And the good-natured dog agreed with me smilingly. It was the most despicable fix. I must plainly content myself with the pack for *Modestine*, and take the following items for my own share of the portage: a cane, a quart flask, a pilot-jacket heavily weighted in the pockets, two pounds of black bread, and an open basket full of meats and bottles. I believe I may say I am not devoid of greatness of soul; for I did not recoil from this infamous burden. I disposed it, Heaven knows how, so as to be mildly portable, and then proceeded to steer *Modestine* through the village. She tried, as was indeed her invariable habit, to enter every house and every courtyard in the whole length; and, encumbered as I was, without a hand to help myself, no words can render an idea of my difficulties. A priest, with six or seven others, was examining a church in process of repair, and he and his acolytes laughed loudly as they saw my plight. I remembered having laughed myself when I had seen good men struggling with adversity in the person of a jackass, and the recollection filled me with penitence. That was in my old light days, before this trouble came upon me. God knows at least that I shall never laugh again, thought I. But O, what a cruel thing is a farce to those engaged in it!

A little out of the village, *Modestine,* filled with the demon, set her heart upon a by-road, and positively refused to leave it. I dropped all my bundles, and, I am ashamed to say, struck the poor sinner twice across the face. It was pitiful to see her lift up her head with shut eyes, as if waiting for another blow. I came very near crying; but I did a wiser thing than that, and sat squarely down by the roadside to consider my situation under the cheerful influence of tobacco and a nip of brandy. *Modestine,* in the mean while, munched some black bread with a contrite hypocritical air. It was plain that I must make a sacrifice to the gods of shipwreck. I threw away the empty bottle destined to carry milk; I threw away my own white bread, and, disdaining to act by general average, kept the black bread for *Modestine;* lastly, I threw away the cold leg of mutton and the egg-whisk, although this last was dear to my heart. Thus I found room for everything in the basket, and even stowed the boating-coat on the top. By means of an end of cord I slung it under one arm; and although the cord cut my shoulder, and the jacket hung almost to the ground, it was with a heart greatly lightened that I set forth again.

I had now an arm free to thrash *Modestine,* and cruelly I chastised her. If I were to reach the lakeside before dark, she must bestir her little shanks to some tune. Already the sun had gone down into a windy-looking mist; and although there were still a few streaks of gold far off to the east on the hills and the black firwoods, all was cold and gray about our onward path. An infinity of little country by-roads led hither and thither among the fields. It was the most pointless labyrinth. I could see my destination overhead, or rather the peak that dominates it; but

choose as I pleased, the roads always ended by turning
away from it, and sneaking back towards the valley, or
northward along the margin of the hills. The failing light,
the waning color, the naked, unhomely, stony country
through which I was travelling, threw me into some despondency. I promise you, the stick was not idle; I think
every decent step that *Modestine* took must have cost me
at least two emphatic blows. There was not another sound
in the neighborhood but that of my unwearying bastinado.

Suddenly, in the midst of my toils, the load once more
bit the dust, and, as by enchantment, all the cords were
simultaneously loosened, and the road scattered with my
dear possessions. The packing was to begin again from
the beginning; and as I had to invent a new and better system, I do not doubt but I lost half an hour. It began to
be dusk in earnest as I reached a wilderness of turf and
stones. It had the air of being a road which should lead
everywhere at the same time; and I was falling into something not unlike despair when I saw two figures stalking
towards me over the stones. They walked one behind the
other like tramps, but their pace was remarkable. The
son led the way, a tall, ill-made, sombre, Scotch-looking
man; the mother followed, all in her Sunday's best, with
an elegantly-embroidered ribbon to her cap, and a new
felt hat atop, and proffering, as she strode along with kilted petticoats, a string of obscene and blasphemous oaths.

I hailed the son and asked him my direction. He pointed loosely west and north-west, muttered an inaudible
comment, and, without slacking his pace for an instant,
stalked on, as he was going, right athwart my path. The
mother followed without so much as raising her head. I

shouted and shouted after them, but they continued to
scale the hillside, and turned a deaf ear to my outcries. At
last, leaving *Modestine* by herself, I was constrained to
run after them, hailing the while. They stopped as I drew
near, the mother still cursing; and I could see she was a
handsome, motherly, respectable-looking woman. The son
once more answered me roughly and inaudibly, and was
for setting out again. But this time I simply collared the
mother, who was nearest me, and, apologizing for my violence, declared that I could not let them go until they had
put me on my road. They were neither of them offended
—rather mollified than otherwise; told me I had only to
follow them; and then the mother asked me what I wanted by the lake at such an hour. I replied, in the Scotch
manner, by inquiring if she had far to go herself. She told
me, with another oath, that she had an hour and a half's
road before her. And then, without salutation, the pair
strode forward again up the hillside in the gathering dusk.

I returned for *Modestine*, pushed her briskly forward,
and, after a sharp ascent of twenty minutes, reached the
edge of a plateau. The view, looking back on my day's
journey, was both wild and sad. *Mount Mézenc* and the
peaks beyond *St. Julien* stood out in trenchant gloom
against a cold glitter in the east; and the intervening field
of hills had fallen together into one broad wash of shadow,
except here and there the outline of a wooded sugar-loaf
in black, here and there a white irregular patch to repre-
sent a cultivated farm, and here and there a blot where
the *Loire,* the *Gazeille,* or the *Lausonne* wandered in a
gorge.

Soon we were on a high-road, and surprise seized on my
mind as I beheld a village of some magnitude close at

hand; for I had been told that the neighborhood of the lake was uninhabited except by trout. The road smoked in the twilight with children driving home cattle from the fields; and a pair of mounted stride-legged women, hat and cap and all, dashed past me at a hammering trot from the canton where they had been to church and market. I asked one of the children where I was. At *Bouchet St. Nicolas,* he told me. Thither, about a mile south of my destination, and on the other side of a respectable summit, had these confused roads and treacherous peasantry conducted me. My shoulder was cut, so that it hurt sharply; my arm arched like toothache from perpetual beating; I gave up the lake and my design to camp, and asked for the *auberge.*

I HAVE A GOAD

THE *auberge* of *Bouchet St. Nicolas* was among the least pretentious I have ever visited; but I saw many more of the like upon my journey. Indeed, it was typical of these French highlands. Imagine a cottage of two stories, with a bench before the door; the stable and kitchen in a *suite,* so that *Modestine* and I could hear each other dining; furniture of the plainest, earthen floors, a single bedchamber for travellers, and that without any convenience but beds. In the kitchen cooking and eating go forward side by side, and the family sleep at night. Any one who has a fancy to wash must do so in public at the common table. The food is sometimes spare; hard fish and omelette have been my portion more than once; the wine is of the smallest, the brandy abominable to man; and the visit of a fat sow, grouting under the table and rubbing against your legs, is no impossible accompaniment to dinner.

But the people of the inn, in nine cases out of ten, show themselves friendly and considerate. As soon as you cross the doors you cease to be a stranger; and although this peasantry are rude and forbidding on the highway, they show a tincture of kind breeding when you share their hearth. At *Bouchet,* for instance, I uncorked my bottle of Beaujolais, and asked the host to join me. He would take but little.

"I am an amateur of such wine, do you see?" he said, "and I am capable of leaving you not enough."

In these hedge-inns the traveller is expected to eat with his own knife; unless he ask, no other will be supplied: with a glass, a whang of bread, and an iron fork, the table is completely laid. My knife was cordially admired by the landlord of *Bouchet,* and the spring filled him with wonder.

"I should never have guessed that," he said. "I would bet," he added, weighing it in his hand, "that this cost you not less than five francs."

When I told him it had cost me twenty, his jaw dropped.

He was a mild, handsome, sensible, friendly old man, astonishingly ignorant. His wife, who was not so pleasant in her manners, knew how to read, although I do not suppose she ever did so. She had a share of brains and spoke with a cutting emphasis, like one who ruled the roost.

"My man knows nothing," she said, with an angry nod; "he is like the beasts."

And the old gentleman signified acquiescence with his head. There was no contempt on her part, and no shame on his; the facts were accepted loyally, and no more about the matter.

I was tightly cross-examined about my journey; and the lady understood in a moment, and sketched out what I should put into my book when I got home. "Whether people harvest or not in such or such a place; if there were forests; studies of manners; what, for example, I and the master of the house say to you; the beauties of Nature, and all that." And she interrogated me with a look.

"It is just that," said I.

"You see," she added to her husband, "I understood that."

They were both much interested by the story of my misadventures.

"In the morning," said the husband, "I will make you something better than your cane. Such a beast as that feels nothing; it is in the proverb—*dur comme un âne;* you might beat her insensible with a cudgel, and yet you would arrive at nowhere."

Something better! I little knew what he was offering.

The sleeping-room was furnished with two beds. I had one; and I will own I was a little abashed to find a young man and his wife and child in the act of mounting into the other. This was my first experience of the sort; and if I am always to feel equally silly and extraneous, I pray God it be my last as well. I kept my eyes to myself, and know nothing of the woman except that she had beautiful arms and seemed no whit abashed by my appearance. As a matter of fact, the situation was more trying to me than to the pair. A pair keep each other in countenance; it is the single gentleman who has to blush. But I could not help attributing my sentiments to the husband, and sought to conciliate his tolerance with a cup of brandy from my flask. He told me that he was a cooper of *Alais* travelling to *St. Etienne* in search of work, and that in his spare moments he followed the fatal calling of a maker of matches. Me he readily enough divined to be a brandy merchant.

I was up first in the morning (*Monday, September 23d*), and hastened my toilet guiltily, so as to leave a clear field for madam, the cooper's wife. I drank a bowl of milk, and set off to explore the neighborhood of *Bouchet*.

It was perishing cold, a gray, windy, wintry morning; misty clouds flew fast and low; the wind piped over the naked platform; and the only speck of color was away behind *Mount Mézenc* and the eastern hills, where the sky still wore the orange of the dawn.

It was five in the morning, and four thousand feet above the sea; and I had to bury my hands in my pockets and trot. People were trooping out to the labors of the field by twos and threes, and all turned round to stare upon the stranger. I had seen them coming back last night, I saw them going afield again; and there was the life of *Bouchet* in a nutshell.

When I came back to the inn for a bit of breakfast, the landlady was in the kitchen combing out her daughter's hair; and I made her my compliments upon its beauty.

"O no," said the mother; "it is not so beautiful as it ought to be. Look, it is too fine."

Thus does a wise peasantry console itself under adverse physical circumstances, and, by a startling democratic process, the defects of the majority decide the type of beauty.

"And where," said I, "is monsieur?"

"The master of the house is up-stairs," she answered, "making you a goad."

Blessed be the man who invented goads! Blessed the innkeeper of *Bouchet St. Nicolas,* who introduced me to their use! This plain wand, with an eighth of an inch of pin, was indeed a sceptre when he put it in my hands. Thenceforward *Modestine* was my slave. A prick, and she passed the most inviting stable-door. A prick, and she broke forth into a gallant little trotlet that devoured the miles. It was not a remarkable speed, when all was said; and we took four hours to cover ten miles at the best of it. But what a heavenly change since yesterday! No more wielding of the ugly cudgel; no more flailing with an aching arm; no more broadsword exercise, but a discreet and gentlemanly fence. And what although now and then a drop of blood should appear on *Modestine's* mouse-coloured wedge-like rump? I should have preferred it otherwise, indeed; but yesterday's exploits had purged my heart of all humanity. The perverse little devil, since she would not be taken with kindness, must even go with pricking.

It was bleak and bitter cold, and, except a cavalcade of stride-legged ladies and a pair of post-runners, the road was dead solitary all the way to *Pradelles*. I scarce remember an incident but one. A handsome foal with a bell about his neck came charging up to us upon a stretch of common, sniffed the air martially as one about to do great deeds, and, suddenly thinking otherwise in his green young heart, put about and galloped off as he had come, the bell tinkling in the wind. For a long while afterwards I saw his noble attitude as he drew up, and heard the note of his bell; and when I struck the highroad, the song of the telegraph-wires seemed to continue the same music.

Pradelles stands on a hillside, high above the *Allier*, surrounded by rich meadows. They were cutting aftermath on all sides, which gave the neighborhood, this gusty autumn morning, an untimely smell of hay. On the opposite bank of the *Allier* the land kept mounting for miles to the horizon: a tanned and sallow autumn landscape, with black blots of fir-wood and white roads wandering through the hills. Over all this the clouds shed a uniform and purplish shadow, sad and somewhat menacing, exaggerating height and distance, and throwing into still higher relief the twisted ribbons of the highway. It was a cheerless prospect, but one stimulating to a traveller. For I was now upon the limit of *Velay,* and all that I beheld lay in another county—wild *Gévaudan,* mountainous, uncultivated, and but recently disforested from terror of the wolves.

Wolves, alas, like bandits, seem to flee the traveller's advance; and you may trudge through all our comfortable Europe, and not meet with an adventure worth the name. But here, if anywhere, a man was on the frontiers of hope. For this was the land of the ever-memorable BEAST, the *Napoléon Buonaparte* of wolves. What a career was his! He lived ten months at free quarters in *Gévaudan* and *Vivarais;* he ate women and children and "shepherdesses celebrated for their beauty"; he pursued armed horsemen; he has been seen at broad noonday chasing a post-chaise and outrider along the king's high-road, and chaise and outrider fleeing before him at the gallop. He was placarded like a political offender, and ten thousand francs were offered for his head. And yet, when he was shot and sent to Versailles, behold! a common wolf, and even small for that. "Though I could reach from pole to pole," sang *Alexander Pope;* the little corporal shook *Europe;* and if all wolves had been as this wolf, they would have changed the history of man. *M. Elie Berthet* has made him the hero of a novel, which I have read, and do not wish to read again.

I hurried over my lunch, and was proof against the landlady's desire that I should visit our *Lady of Pradelles,* "who performed many miracles, although she was of wood"; and before three quarters of an hour I was goading *Modestine* down the steep descent that leads to *Lan-*

gogne on the *Allier*. On both sides of the road, in big
dusty fields, farmers were preparing for next spring. Every
fifty yards a yoke of great-necked stolid oxen were patiently haling at the plough. I saw one of these mild, formid-
able servants of the glebe, who took a sudden interest in
Modestine and me. The furrow down which he was
journeying lay at an angle to the road, and his head was
solidly fixed to the yoke like those of caryatides below a
ponderous cornice; but he screwed round his big honest
eyes and followed us with a ruminating look, until his
master bade him turn the plough and proceed to reascend
the field. From all these furrowing ploughshares, from
the feet of oxen, from a laborer here and there who was
breaking the dry clods with a hoe, the wind carried away
a thin dust like so much smoke. It was a fine, busy,
breathing, rustic landscape; and as I continued to descend, the highlands of *Gévaudan* kept mounting in front
of me against the sky.

I had crossed the *Loire* the day before; now I was to
cross the *Allier;* so near are these two confluents in their
youth. Just at the bridge of *Langogne,* as the long-
promised rain was beginning to fall, a lassie of some seven
or eight addressed me in the sacramental phrase, *"D'où'st
que vous venez?"* She did it with so high an air that she
set me laughing; and this cut her to the quick. She was
evidently one who reckoned on respect, and stood looking
after me in silent dudgeon, as I crossed the bridge and
entered the county of *Gévaudan*.

UPPER GEVAUDAN

"The way also here was very wearisome through dirt
and slabbiness; nor was there on all this ground so much
as one inn or victualling-house wherein to refresh the
feebler sort."—*Pilgrim's Progress.*

UPPER GEVAUDAN

A CAMP IN THE DARK

THE next day (*Tuesday, September 24th*), it was two o'clock in the afternoon before I got my journal written up and my knapsack repaired, for I was deter mined to carry my knapsack in the future and have no more ado with baskets; and half an hour afterwards I set out for *Le Cheylard l'Evêque*, a place on the borders of the forest of *Mercoire*. A man, I was told, should walk there in an hour and a half; and I thought it scarce too ambitious to suppose that a man encumbered with a donkey might cover the same distance in four hours.

All the way up the long hill from *Langogne* it rained and hailed alternately; the wind kept freshening steadily, although slowly; plentiful hurrying clouds—some drag-ging veils of straight rain-shower, others massed and lum-inous, as though promising snow—careered out of the north and followed me along my way. I was soon out of the cultivated basin of the *Allier*, and away from the ploughing oxen, and suchlike sights of the country. Moor, heathery marsh, tracts of rock and pines, woods of birch all jewelled with the autumn yellow, here and there a few naked cottages and bleak fields,—these were the charac-ters of the country. Hill and valley followed valley and hill; the little green and stony cattle-tracks wandered in and out of one another, split into three or four, died away in marshy hollows, and began again sporadically on hillsides or at the borders of a wood.

There was no direct road to *Cheylard,* and it was no easy affair to make a passage in this uneven country and through this intermittent labyrinth of tracks. It must have been about four when I struck *Sagnerousse,* and went on my way rejoicing in a sure point of departure. Two hours afterwards, the dusk rapidly falling, in a lull of the wind, I issued from a fir-wood where I had long been wandering, and found, not the looked-for village, but another marish bottom among rough-and-tumble hills. For some time past I had heard the ringing of cattle-bells ahead; and now, as I came out of the skirts of the wood, I saw near upon a dozen cows and perhaps as many more black figures, which I conjectured to be children, although the mist had almost unrecognizably exaggerated their forms. These were all silently following each other round and round in a circle, now taking hands, now breaking up with chains and reverences. A dance of children appeals to very innocent and lively thoughts; but, at nightfall on the marshes, the thing was eerie and fantastic to behold. Even I, who am well enough read in *Herbert Spencer,* felt a sort of silence fall for an instant on my mind. The next I was pricking *Modestine* forward, and guiding her like an unruly ship through the open. In a path, she went doggedly ahead of her own accord, as before a fair wind; but once on the turf or among heather, and the brute became demented. The tendency of lost travellers to go round in a circle was developed in her to the degree of passion, and it took all the steering I had in me to keep even a decently straight course through a single field.

While I was thus desperately tacking through the bog,

children and cattle began to disperse, until only a pair of girls remained behind. From these I sought direction on my path. The peasantry in general were but little disposed to counsel a wayfarer. One old devil simply retired into his house, and barricaded the door on my approach; and I might beat and shout myself hoarse, he turned a deaf ear. Another, having given me a direction which, as I found afterwards, I had misunderstood, complacently watched me going wrong without adding a sign. He did not care a stalk of parsley if I wandered all night upon the hills! As for these two girls, they were a pair of impudent sly sluts, with not a thought but mischief. One put out her tongue at me, the other bade me follow the cows; and they both giggled and jogged each other's elbows. The Beast of *Gévaudan* ate about a hundred children of this district; I began to think of him with sympathy.

Leaving the girls, I pushed on through the bog, and got into another wood and upon a well-marked road. It grew darker and darker. *Modestine,* suddenly beginning to smell mischief, bettered the pace of her own accord, and from that time forward gave me no trouble. It was the first sign of intelligence I had occasion to remark in her. At the same time, the wind freshened into half a gale, and another heavy discharge of rain came flying up out of the north. At the other side of the wood I sighted some red windows in the dusk. This was the hamlet of *Fouzilhic;* three houses on a hillside, near a wood of birches. Here I found a delightful old man, who came a little way with me in the rain to put me safely on the road for *Cheylard.* He would hear of no reward; but shook his hands above his head almost as if in menace, and refused volubly and shrilly. in unmitigated *patois.*

All seemed right at last. My thoughts began to turn upon dinner and a fireside, and my heart was agreeably softened in my bosom. Alas, and I was on the brink of new and greater miseries! Suddenly, at a single swoop, the night fell. I have been abroad in many a black night, but never in a blacker. A glimmer of rocks, a glimmer of the track where it was well beaten, a certain fleecy density, or night within night, for a tree,—this was all that I could discriminate. The sky was simply darkness overhead; even the flying clouds pursued their way invisibly to human eyesight. I could not distinguish my hand at arm's length from the track, nor my goad, at the same distance, from the meadows or the sky.

Soon the road that I was following split, after the fashion of the country, into three or four in a piece of rocky meadow. Since *Modestine* had shown such a fancy for beaten roads, I tried her instinct in this predicament. But the instinct of an ass is what might be expected from the name; in half a minute she was clambering round and round among some boulders, as lost a donkey as you would wish to see. I should have camped long before had I been properly provided; but as this was to be so short a stage, I had brought no wine, no bread for myself, and a little over a pound for my lady-friend. Add to this, that I and *Modestine* were both handsomely wetted by the showers. But now, if I could have found some water, I should have camped at once in spite of all. Water, however, being entirely absent, except in the form of rain, I determined to return to *Fouzilhic,* and ask a guide a little further on my way—"a little farther lend thy guiding hand."

The thing was easy to decide, hard to accomplish. In

this sensible roaring blackness I was sure of nothing but the direction of the wind. To this I set my face; the road had disappeared, and I went across country, now in marshy opens, now baffled by walls unscalable to *Modestine,* until I came once more in sight of some red windows. This time they were differently disposed. It was not *Fouzilhic,* but *Fouzilhac,* a hamlet little distant from the other in space, but worlds away in the spirit of its inhabitants. I tied *Modestine* to a gate, and groped forward, stumbling among rocks, plunging mid-leg in bog, until I gained the entrance of the village. In the first lighted house there was a woman who would not open to me. She could do nothing, she cried to me through the door, being alone and lame; but if I would apply at the next house, there was a man who could help me if he had a mind.

They came to the next door in force, a man, two women, and a girl, and brought a pair of lanterns to examine the wayfarer. The man was not ill-looking, but had a shifty smile. He leaned against the doorpost, and heard me state my case. All I asked was a guide as far as *Cheylard.*

"*C'est que, voyez-vous, il fait noir,*" said he.

I told him that was just my reason for requiring help. "I understand that," said he, looking uncomfortable; "*mais—c'est—de la peine.*"

I was willing to pay, I said. He shook his head. I rose as high as ten francs; but he continued to shake his head. "Name your own price, then," said I.

"*Ce n'est pas ça,*" he said at length, and with evident difficulty; "but I am not going to cross the door—*mais je ne sortirai pas de la porte.*"

I grew a little warm, and asked him what he proposed that I should do.

"Where are you going beyond *Cheylard?*" he asked by way of answer.

"That is no affair of yours," I returned, for I was not going to indulge his bestial curiosity; "it changes nothing in my present predicament."

"*C'est vrai, ça,*" he acknowledged with a laugh; "*oui, c'est vrai. Et d'où venez-vous?*"

A better man than I might have felt nettled.

"O," said I, "I am not going to answer any of your questions, so you may spare yourself the trouble of putting them. I am late enough already; I want help. If you will not guide me yourself, at least help me to find some one else who will."

"Hold on," he cried suddenly. "Was it not you who passed in the meadow while it was still day?"

"Yes, yes," said the girl, whom I had not hitherto recognized; "it was monsieur, I told him to follow the cow."

"As for you, mademoiselle," said I, "you are a *farceuse.*"

"And," added the man, "what the devil have you done to be still here?"

What the devil, indeed! But there I was. "The great thing," said I, "is to make an end of it;" and once more proposed that he should help me to find a guide.

"*C'est que,*" he said again, "*c'est que—il fait noir.*"

"Very well," said I; "take one of your lanterns."

"No," he cried, drawing a thought backward, and again intrenching himself behind one of his former phrases; "I will not cross the door."

I looked at him. I saw unaffected terror struggling on his face with unaffected shame; he was smiling pitifully

and wetting his lip with his tongue, like a detected schoolboy. I drew a brief picture of my state, and asked him
what I was to do.

"I don't know," he said; "I will not cross the door."

Here was the Beast of *Gévaudan,* and no mistake.

"Sir," said I, with my most commanding manners, "you
are a coward."

And with that I turned my back upon the family party,
who hastened to retire within their fortifications; and the
famous door was closed again, but not till I had overheard
the sound of laughter. *Filia barbara pater barbarior.* Let
me say it in the plural: the Beasts of *Gévaudan.*

The lanterns had somewhat dazzled me, and I ploughed
distressfully among stones and rubbish-heaps. All the
other houses in the village were both dark and silent; and
though I knocked at here and there a door, my knocking
was unanswered. It was a bad business; I gave up *Fouzilhac* with my curses. The rain had stopped, and the
wind, which still kept rising, began to dry my coat and
trousers. "Very well," thought I, "water or no water, I
must camp." But the first thing was to return to *Modestine.* I am pretty sure I was twenty minutes groping for my
lady in the dark; and if it had not been for the unkindly
services of the bog, into which I once more stumbled, I
might have still been groping for her at the dawn. My next
business was to gain the shelter of a wood, for the wind
was cold as well as boisterous. How, in this well-wooded
district, I should have been so long in finding one, is another of the insoluble mysteries of this day's adventures;
but I will take my oath that I put near an hour to the discovery.

At last black trees began to show up on my left, and sud-

denly crossing the road, made a cave of unmitigated blackness right in front. I call it a cave without exaggeration;
to pass below that arch of leaves was like entering a dun-
geon. I felt about until my hand encountered a stout
branch, and to this I tied *Modestine,* a haggard, drenched,
desponding donkey. Then I lowered my pack, laid it along
the wall on the margin of the road, and unbuckled the
straps. I knew well enough where the lantern was; but
where were the candles? I groped and groped among the
tumbled articles, and, while I was thus groping, suddenly
I touched the spirit-lamp. Salvation! This would serve
my turn as well. The wind roared unwearyingly among
the trees; I could hear the boughs tossing and the leaves
churning through half a mile of forest; yet the scene of my
encampment was not only as black as the pit, but admir-
ably sheltered. At the second match the wick caught
flame. The light was both livid and shifting; but it cut
me off from the universe, and doubled the darkness of the
surrounding night.

I tied *Modestine* more conveniently for herself, and
broke up half the black bread for her supper, reserving
the other half against the morning. Then I gathered what
I should want within reach, took off my wet boots and
gaiters, which I wrapped in my waterproof, arranged my
knapsack for a pillow under the flap of my sleeping-bag,
insinuated my limbs into the interior, and buckled myself
in like a bambino. I opened a tin of Bologna sausage and
broke a cake of chocolate, and that was all I had to eat. It
may sound offensive, but I ate them together, bite by bite,
by way of bread and meat. All I had to wash down this
revolting mixture was neat brandy: a revolting beverage in
itself. But I was rare and hungry; ate well, and smoked

one of the best cigarettes in my experience. Then I put a
stone in my straw hat, pulled the flap of my fur cap over
my neck and eyes, put my revolver ready to my hand, and
snuggled well down among the sheepskins.

I questioned at first if I were sleepy, for I felt my heart
beating faster than usual, as if with an agreeable excitement to which my mind remained a stranger. But as soon
as my eyelids touched, that subtle glue leaped between
them, and they would no more come separate. The wind
among the trees was my lullaby. Sometimes it sounded
for minutes together with a steady even rush, not rising
nor abating; and again it would swell and burst like a
great crashing breaker, and the trees would patter me all
over with big drops from the rain of the afternoon. Night
after night, in my own bedroom in the country, I have
given ear to this perturbing concert of the wind among
the woods; but whether it was a difference in the trees, or
the lie of the ground, or because I was myself outside and
in the midst of it, the fact remains that the wind sang to
a different tune among these woods of *Gévaudan*. I hearkened and hearkened; and meanwhile sleep took gradual
possession of my body and subdued my thoughts and
senses; but still my last waking effort was to listen and
distinguish, and my last conscious state was one of wonder
at the foreign clamor in my ears.

Twice in the course of the dark hours—once when a
stone galled me underneath the sack, and again when the
poor patient *Modestine,* growing angry, pawed and stamped upon the road—I was recalled for a brief while to consciousness, and saw a star or two overhead, and the lace-
like edge of the foliage against the sky. When I awoke
for the third time (*Wednesday, September* 25*th*), the

world was flooded with a blue light, the mother of the dawn. I saw the leaves laboring in the wind and the ribbon of the road; and, on turning my head, there was *Modestine* tied to a beech, and standing half across the path in an attitude of inimitable patience. I closed my eyes again, and set to thinking over the experience of the night. I was surprised to find how easy and pleasant it had been, even in this tempestuous weather. The stone which annoyed me would not have been there, had I not been forced to camp blindfold in the opaque night; and I had felt no other inconvenience, except when my feet encountered the lantern or the second volume of *Peyrat's Pastors of the Desert* among the mixed contents of my sleeping-bag; nay more, I had felt not a touch of cold, and awakened with unusually lightsome and clear sensations.

With that, I shook myself, got once more into my boots and gaiters, and, breaking up the rest of the bread for *Modestine,* strolled about to see in what part of the world I had awakened. *Ulysses,* left on *Ithaca,* and with a mind unsettled by the goddess, was not more pleasantly astray. I have been after an adventure all my life, a pure dispassionate adventure, such as befell early and heroic voyagers; and thus to be found by morning in a random woodside nook in *Gévaudan*—not knowing north from south, as strange to my surroundings as the first man upon the earth, an inland castaway—was to find a fraction of my day-dreams realized. I was on the skirts of a little wood of birch, sprinkled with a few beeches; behind, it adjoined another wood of fir; and in front, it broke up and went down in open order into a shallow and meadowy dale. All around there were bare hill-tops, some near, some far away, as the perspective closed and opened, but none apparently much higher than the rest. The wind huddled the trees. The golden specks of autumn in the birches tossed shiveringly. Overhead the sky was full of strings and shreds of vapor, flying, vanishing, reappearing, and turning about an axis like tumblers, as the wind hounded them through heaven. It was wild weather and famishing cold. I ate some chocolate, swallowed a mouthful of brandy, and smoked a cigarette before the cold should have time to disable my fingers. And by the time I had got all this done, and had made my pack and bound it on the pack-saddle, the day was tiptoe on the threshold of the east. We had not gone many steps along the lane, before the sun, still invisible to me, sent a glow of gold over some cloud mountains that lay ranged along the eastern sky.

The wind had us on the stern, and hurried us bitingly forward. I buttoned myself into my coat, and walked on in a pleasant frame of mind with all men, when suddenly, at a corner, there was *Fouzilhic* once more in front of me. Nor only that, but there was the old gentleman who had escorted me so far the night before, running out of his house at sight of me, with hands upraised in horror.

"My poor boy!" he cried, "what does this mean?"

I told him what had happened. He beat his old hands like clappers in a mill, to think how lightly he had let me go; but when he heard of the man of *Fouzilhac*, anger and depression seized upon his mind.

"This time, at least," said he, "there shall be no mistake."

And he limped along, for he was very rheumatic, for about half a mile, and until I was almost within sight of *Cheylard*, the destination I had hunted for so long.

CHEYLARD AND LUC

CANDIDLY, it seemed little worthy of all this searching. A few broken ends of village, with no particular street, but a succession of open places heaped with
logs and fagots; a couple of tilted crosses, a shrine to our
Lady of all Graces on the summit of a little hill; and all
this, upon a rattling highland river, in the corner of a
naked valley. What went ye out for to see? thought I to
myself. But the place had a life of its own. I found a
board commemorating the liberalities of *Cheylard* for the
past year, hung up, like a banner, in the diminutive and
tottering church. In 1877, it appeared, the inhabitants
subscribed forty-eight francs ten centimes for the "Work
of the Propagation of the Faith." Some of this, I could
not help hoping, would be applied to my native land.
Cheylard scrapes together half-pence for the darkened
souls in *Edinburgh;* while *Balquidder* and *Dunrossness*
bemoan the ignorance of *Rome*. Thus, to the high entertainment of the angels, do we pelt each other with evange-
lists, like school-boys bickering in the snow.

The inn was again singularly unpretentious. The whole
furniture of a not ill-to-do family was in the kitchen: the
beds, the cradle, the clothes, the plate-rack, the meal-chest,
and the photograph of the parish priest. There were five
children, one of whom was set to its morning prayers at
the stair-foot soon after my arrival, and a sixth would
erelong be forthcoming. I was kindly received by these

good folk. They were much interested in my misadventure. The wood in which I had slept belonged to them; the man of *Fouzilhac* they thought a monster of iniquity, and counselled me warmly to summon him at law—"because I might have died." The good wife was horror-stricken to see me drink over a pint of uncreamed milk.

"You will do yourself an evil," she said. "Permit me to boil it for you."

After I had begun the morning on this delightful liquor, she having an infinity of things to arrange, I was permitted, nay requested, to make a bowl of chocolate for myself. My boots and gaiters were hung up to dry, and, seeing me trying to write my journal on my knee, the eldest daughter let down a hinged table in the chimney-corner for my convenience. Here I wrote, drank my chocolate, and finally ate an omelette before I left. The table was thick with dust; for, as they explained, it was not used except in winter weather. I had a clear look up the vent, through brown agglomerations of soot and blue vapor, to the sky; and whenever a handful of twigs was thrown on to the fire, my legs were scorched by the blaze.

The husband had begun life as a muleteer, and when I came to charge *Modestine* showed himself full of the prudence of his art. "You will have to change this package," said he; "it ought to be in two parts, and then you might have double the weight."

I explained that I wanted no more weight; and for no donkey hitherto created would I cut my sleeping-bag in two.

"It fatigues her, however," said the innkeeper; "it fatigues her greatly on the march. Look."

Alas, there were her two forelegs no better than raw

beef on the inside, and blood was running from under her tail. They told me when I left, and I was ready to believe it, that before a few days I should come to love *Modestine* like a dog. Three days had passed, we had shared some misadventures, and my heart was still as cold as a potato towards my beast of burden. She was pretty enough to look at; but then she had given proof of dead stupidity, redeemed indeed by patience, but aggravated by flashes of sorry and ill-judged light-heartedness. And I own this new discovery seemed another point against her. What the devil was the good of a she-ass if she could not carry a sleeping-bag and a few necessaries? I saw the end of the fable rapidly approaching, when I should have to carry *Modestine*. *Æsop* was the man to know the world! I assure you I set out with heavy thoughts upon my short day's march.

It was not only heavy thoughts about *Modestine* that weighted me upon the way; it was a leaden business altogether. For first, the wind blew so rudely that I had to hold on the pack with one hand from *Cheyland* to *Luc;* and second, my road lay through one of the most beggarly countries in the world. It was like the worst of the Scotch Highlands, only worse; cold, naked, and ignoble, scant of wood, scant of heather, scant of life. A road and some fences broke the unvarying waste, and the line of the road was marked by upright pillars, to serve in time of snow.

Why any one should desire to visit either *Luc* or *Cheylard* is more than my much-inventing spirit can suppose. For my part, I travel not to go anywhere, but to go. I travel for travel's sake. The great affair is to move; to feel the needs and hitches of our life more nearly; to come down off this feather-bed of civilization, and find the globe granite underfoot and strewn with cutting flints. Alas, as we get up in life, and are more preoccupied with our affairs, even a holiday is a thing that must be worked for. To hold a pack upon a pack-saddle against a gale out of the freezing north is no high industry, but it is one that serves to occupy and compose the mind. And when the present is so exacting, who can annoy himself about the future?

I came out at length above the *Allier*. A more unsightly prospect at this season of the year it would be hard to fancy. Shelving hills rose round it on all sides, here dabbled with wood and fields, there rising to peaks alternately naked and hairy with pines. The color throughout was black or ashen, and came to a point in the ruins of the castle of *Luc,* which pricked up impudently from below my feet, carrying on a pinnacle a tall white statue of our Lady, which I heard with interest, weighed fifty quintals, and was to be dedicated on the 6th of *October.* Through this sorry landscape trickled the *Allier* and a tributary of nearly equal size, which came down to join it through a broad nude valley in *Viverais.* The weather had somewhat lightened, and the clouds massed in squadron; but the fierce wind still hunted them through heaven, and cast great ungainly splashes of shadow and sunlight over the scene.

Luc itself was a straggling double file of houses wedged between hill and river. It had no beauty, nor was there any notable feature, save the old castle overhead with its fifty quintals of brand-new Madonna. But the inn was clean and large. The kitchen, with its two box-beds hung with clean check curtains, with its wide stone chimney, its chimney-shelf four yards long and garnished with lanterns and religious statuettes, its array of chests and pair of ticking clocks, was the very model of what a kitchen ought to be; a melodrama kitchen, suitable for bandits or noblemen in disguise. Nor was the scene disgraced by the landlady, a handsome, silent, dark old woman, clothed and hooded in black like a nun. Even the public bedroom had a character of its own, with the long deal tables and benches, where fifty might have dined, set out as for a harvest-home, and the three box-beds along the wall. In one of these, lying on straw and covered with a pair of table-napkins, did I do penance all night long in gooseflesh and chattering teeth, and sigh from time to time as I awakened for my sheepskin sack and the lee of some great wood.

OUR LADY OF THE SNOWS

"I behold
The House, the Brotherhood austere—
And what am I, that I am here?"
MATTHEW ARNOLD.

OUR LADY OF THE SNOWS

FATHER APOLLINARIS

NEXT morning (*Thursday, 26th September*) I took
the road in a new order. The sack was no longer
doubled, but hung at full length across the saddle, a green
sausage six feet long with a tuft of blue wool hanging out
of either end. It was more picturesque, it spared the
donkey, and, as I began to see, it would insure stability,
blow high, blow low. But it was not without a pang that I
had so decided. For although I had purchased a new cord,
and made all as fast as I was able, I was yet jealously uneasy lest the flaps should tumble out and scatter my effects
along the line of march.

My way lay up the bald valley of the river, along the
march of *Vivarais* and *Gévaudan*. The hills of *Gévaudan*
on the right were a little more naked, if anything, than
those of *Vivarais* upon the left, and the former had a mon-
opoly of a low dotty underwood that grew thickly in the
gorges and died out in solitary burrs upon the shoulders
and the summits. Black bricks of firwood were plastered
here and there upon both sides, and here and there were
cultivated fields. A railway ran beside the river; the only
bit of railway in *Gévaudan*, although there are many pro-
posals afoot and surveys being made, and even, as they tell
me, a station standing ready-built in *Mende*. A year or

two hence and this may be another world. The desert ıs
beleaguered. Now may some Languedocian *Wordsworth*
turn the sonnet into *patois:* "Mountains and vales and
floods, heard YE that whistle?"

At a place called *La Bastide* I was directed to leave the
river, and follow a road that mounted on the left among
the hills of *Vivarais,* the modern *Ardèche;* for I was now
come within a little way of my strange destination, the
Trappist monastery of our *Lady of the Snows.* The sun
came out as I left the shelter of a pine-wood, and I beheld
suddenly a fine wild landscape to the south. High, rocky
hills, as blue as sapphire, closed the view, and between
these lay ridge upon ridge, heathery, craggy, the sun glit-
tering on veins of rock, the underwood clambering in
hollows, as rude as God made them at the first. There
was not a sign of man's hand in all the prospect; and indeed not a trace of his passage, save where generation after
generation had walked in twisted footpaths, in and out
among the beeches, and up and down upon the channelled
slopes. The mists, which had hitherto beset me, were now
broken into clouds, and fled swiftly and shone brightly in
the sun. I drew a long breath. It was grateful to come,
after so long, upon a scene of some attraction for the
human heart. I own I like definite form in what my eyes
are to rest upon; and if landscapes were sold, like the
sheets of characters of my boyhood, one penny plain and
twopence colored, I should go the length of twopence
every day of my life.

But if things had grown better to the south, it was still
desolate and inclement near at hand. A spidery cross on
every hill-top marked the neighborhood of a religious
house; and a quarter of a mile beyond, the outlook south-

ward opening out and growing bolder with every step, a
white statue of the Virgin at the corner of a young planta-
tion directed the traveller to our *Lady of the Snows*. Here,
then, I struck leftward, and pursued my way, driving my
secular donkey before me, and creaking in my secular
boots and gaiters, towards the asylum of silence.

I had not gone very far ere the wind brought to me the
clanging of a bell, and somehow, I can scarce tell why, my
heart sank within me at the sound. I have rarely approached anything with more unaffected terror than the
monastery of our *Lady of the Snows*. This it is to have
a Protestant education. And suddenly, on turning a corner, fear took hold on me from head to foot—slavish
superstitious fear; and though I did not stop in my advance, yet I went on slowly, like a man who should have
passed a bourne unnoticed, and strayed into the country
of the dead. For there upon the narrow new-made road,
between the stripling pines, was a mediæval friar, fighting
with a barrowful of turfs. Every *Sunday* of my childhood
I used to study the *Hermits of Marco Sadeler*—enchanting
prints, full of wood and field and mediæval landscapes, as
large as a county for the imagination to go a travelling in;
and here, sur enough, was one of *Marco Sadeler's* heroes.
He was robed in white like any spectre, and the hood falling back, in the instancy of his contention with the barrow, disclosed a pate as bald and yellow as a skull. He
might have been buried any time these thousand years,
and all the lively parts of him resolved into earth and
broken up with the farmer's harrow.

I was troubled besides in my mind as to etiquette.
Durst I address a person who was under a vow of silence?
Clearly not. But drawing near, I doffed my cap to him

with a far-away superstitious reverence. He nodded back, and cheerfully addressed me. Was I going to the monastery? Who was I? An Englishman? Ah, an Irishman, then?

"No," I said, "a Scotsman."

A Scotsman? Ah, he had never seen a Scotsman before. And he looked me all over, his good, honest, brawny countenance shining with interest, as a boy might look upon a lion or an alligator. From him I learned with disgust that I could not be received at our *Lady of the Snows;* I might get a meal, perhaps, but that was all. And then as our talk ran on, and it turned out that I was not a pedler, but a literary man, who drew landscapes and was going to write a book, he changed his manner of thinking as to my reception (for I fear they respect persons even in a Trappist monastery), and told me I must be sure to ask for the Father Prior, and state my case to him in full. On second thoughts he determined to go down with me himself; he thought he could manage for me better. Might he say that I was a geographer?

No; I thought, in the interests of truth, he positively might not.

"Very well, then" (with disappointment), "an author."

It appeared he had been in a seminary with six young Irishmen, all priests long since, who had received newspapers and kept him informed of the state of ecclesiastical affairs in England. And he asked me eagerly after *Dr. Pusey,* for whose conversion the good man had continued ever since to pray night and morning.

"I thought he was very near the truth," he said; "and he will reach it yet; there is so much virtue in prayer."

He must be a stiff ungodly Protestant who can take anything but pleasure in this kind and hopeful story. While he was thus near the subject, the good father asked me if I were a Christian; and when he found I was not, or not after his way, he glossed it over with great good-will.

The road which we were following, and which this stalwart father had made with his own two hands within the space of a year, came to a corner, and showed us some white buildings a little further on beyond the wood. At the same time, the bell once more sounded abroad. We were hard upon the monastery. *Father Apollinaris* (for that was my companion's name) stopped me.

"I must not speak to you down there," he said. "Ask for the Brother Porter, and all will be well. But try to see me as you go out again through the wood, where I may speak to you. I am charmed to have made your acquaintance."

And then suddenly raising his arms, flapping his fingers, and crying out twice, "I must not speak, I must not speak!" he ran away in front of me, and disappeared into the monastery-door.

I own this somewhat ghastly eccentricity went a good way to revive my terrors. But where one was so good and simple, why should not all be alike? I took heart of grace, and went forward to the gate as fast as *Modestine,* who seemed to have a disaffection for monasteries, would permit. It was the first door, in my acquaintance of her, which she had not shown an indecent haste to enter. I summoned the place in form, though with a quaking heart. *Father Michael,* the Father Hospitaller, and a pair of brown-robed brothers came to the gate and spoke with me awhile. I think my sack was the great attraction; it had already beguiled the heart of poor *Apollinaris,* who had charged me on my life to show it to the **Father Prior**. But whether it was my address, or the sack, or the idea speedily published among that part of the brotherhood who attend on strangers that I was not a pedler after all, I found no difficulty as to my reception. *Modestine* was led away by a layman to the stables, and I and my pack were received into our *Lady of the Snows*.

THE MONKS

FATHER MICHAEL, a pleasant, fresh-faced, smiling man, perhaps of thirty-five, took me to the pantry, and gave me a glass of liqueur to stay me until dinner. We had some talk, or rather I should say he listened to my prattle indulgently enough, but with an abstracted air, like a spirit with a thing of clay. And truly when I remember that I descanted principally on my appetite, and that it must have been by that time more than eighteen hours since *Father Michael* had so much as broken bread, I can well understand that he would find an earthly savor in my conversation. But his manner, though superior, was exquisitely gracious; and I find I have a lurking curiosity as to *Father Michael's* past.

The whet administered, I was left alone for a little in the monastery garden. This is no more than the main court, laid out in sandy paths and beds of party-colored dahlias, and with a fountain and a black statue of the Virgin in the centre. The buildings stand around it four-square, bleak, as yet unseasoned by the years and weather, and with no other features than a belfry and a pair of slated gables. Brothers in white, brothers in brown, passed silently along the sanded alleys; and when I first came out, three hooded monks were kneeling on the terrace at their prayers. A naked hill commands the monastery upon one side, and the wood commands it on the other. It lies exposed to wind; the snow falls off and on from *October* to *May,* and sometimes lies six weeks on end; but if they stood in *Eden,* with a climate like heaven's, the buildings themselves would offer the same wintry and cheerless aspect; and for my part, on this wild *September* day, before I was called to dinner, I felt chilly in and out.

When I had eaten well and heartily, *Brother Ambrose,* a hearty conversable Frenchman (for all those who wait on strangers have the liberty to speak), led me to a little room in that part of the building which is set apart for *MM. les retraitants.* It was clean and whitewashed, and furnished with strict necessaries, a crucifix, a bust of the late Pope, the *Imitation* in French, a book of religious meditations, and the life of *Elizabeth Seton,* evangelist, it would appear, of *North America* and of *New England* in particular. As far as my experience goes, there is a fair field for some more evangelization in these quarters; but think of *Cotton Mather!* I should like to give him a reading of this little work in heaven, where I hope he dwells; but perhaps he knows all that already, and much more; and perhaps he and *Mrs. Seton* are the dearest friends, and gladly unite their voices in the everlasting psalm. Over the table, to conclude the inventory of the room, hung a set of regulations for *MM. les retraitants:* what services they should attend, when they were to tell their beads or meditate, and when they were to rise and go to rest. At the foot was a notable N. B.: *"Le temps libre est employé à l'examen de conscience, à la confession, à faire de bonnes résolutions,"* &c. To make good resolutions, indeed! You might talk as fruitfully of making the hair grow on your head.

I had scarce explored my niche when *Brother Ambrose*

returned. An English boarder, it appeared, would like to speak with me. I professed my willingness, and the friar ushered in a fresh, young little Irishman of fifty, a deacon of the Church, arrayed in strict canonicals, and wearing on his head what, in default of knowledge, I can only call the ecclesiastical shako. He had lived seven years in retreat at a convent of nuns in *Belgium,* and now five at our *Lady of the Snows;* he never saw an English newspaper; he spoke French imperfectly, and had he spoken it like a native, there was not much chance of conversation where he dwelt. With this, he was a man eminently sociable, greedy of news, and simple-minded like a child. If I was pleased to have a guide about the monastery, he was no less delighted to see an English face and hear an English tongue.

He showed me his own room, where he passed his time among breviaries, Hebrew bibles, and the Waverley novels. Thence he led me to the cloisters, into the chapter--house, through the vestry, where the brothers' gowns and broad straw hats were hanging up, each with his religious name upon a board,—names full of legendary suavity and interest, such as *Basil, Hilarion, Raphael,* or *Pacifique;* into the library, where were all the works of *Veuillot* and *Chateaubriand,* and the *Odes et Ballades,* if you please, and even *Molière,* to say nothing of innumerable fathers and a great variety of local and general historians. Thence my good Irishman took me round the workshops, where brothers bake bread, and make cartwheels, and take photographs; where one superintends a collection of curiosities, and another a gallery of rabbits. For in a Trappist monastery each monk has an occupation of his own choice, apart from his religious duties and the general labors of the

house. Each must sing in the choir, if he has a voice and
ear, and join in the haymaking if he has a hand to stir;
but in his private hours, although he must be occupied, he
may be occupied on what he likes. Thus I was told that
one brother was engaged with literature; while *Father
Apollinaris* busies himself in making roads, and the Abbot
employs himself in binding books. It is not so long since
this Abbot was consecrated, by the way; and on that occasion, by a special grace, his mother was permitted to enter
the chapel and witness the ceremony of consecration. A
proud day for her to have a son a mitred abbot; it makes
you glad to think they let her in.

In all these journeyings to and fro, many silent fathers
and brethren fell in our way. Usually they paid no more
regard to our passage than if we had been a cloud; but
sometimes the good deacon had a permission to ask of
them, and it was granted by a peculiar movement of the
hands, almost like that of a dog's paws in swimming, or refused by the usual negative signs, and in either case with
lowered eyelids and a certain air of contrition, as of a man
who was steering very close to evil.

The monks, by special grace of their Abbot, were still
taking two meals a day; but it was already time for their
grand fast, which begins somewhere in *September* and
lasts till *Easter*, and during which they eat but once in the
twenty-four hours, and that at two in the afternoon,
twelve hours after they have begun the toil and vigil of
the day. Their meals are scanty, but even of these they eat
sparingly; and though each is allowed a small *carafe* of
wine, many refrain from this indulgence. Without doubt,
the most of mankind grossly overeat themselves; our meals
serve not only for support, but as a hearty and natural di-

version from the labor of life. Although excess may be hurtful, I should have thought this Trappist regimen defective. And I am astonished, as I look back, at the freshness of face and cheerfulness of manner of all whom I beheld. A happier nor a healthier company I should scarce suppose that I have ever seen. As a matter of fact, on this bleak upland, and with the incessant occupation of the monks, life is of an uncertain tenure, and death no infrequent visitor, at our *Lady of the Snows*. This, at least, was what they told me. But if they die easily, they must live healthily in the meantime, for they seemed all firm of flesh and high in color; and the only morbid sign that I could observe, an unusual brilliancy of eye, was one that served rather to increase the general impression of vivacity and strength.

Those with whom I spoke were singularly sweet-tempered, with what I can only call a holy cheerfulness in air and conversation. There is a note, in the direction to visitors, telling them not to be offended at the curt speech of those who wait upon them, since it is proper to monks to speak little. The note might have been spared; to a man the hospitallers were all brimming with innocent talk, and, in my experience of the monastery, it was easier to begin than to break off a conversation. With the exception of *Father Michael,* who was a man of the world, they showed themselves full of kind and healthy interest in all sorts of subjects—in politics, in voyages, in my sleeping-sack—and not without a certain pleasure in the sound of their own voices.

As for those who are restricted to silence, I can only wonder how they bear their solemn and cheerless isolation. And yet, apart from any view of mortification, I can see a certain policy, not only in the exclusion of women, but in this vow of silence. I have had some experience of lay phalansteries, of an artistic, not to say a bacchanalian, character; and seen more than one association easily formed and yet more easily dispersed. With a Cistercian rule, perhaps they might have lasted longer. In the neighborhood of women it is but a touch-and-go association that can be formed among defenceless men; stronger electricity is sure to triumph; the dreams of boyhood, the schemes of youth, are abandoned, after an interview of ten minutes, and the arts and sciences, and professional male jollity, deserted at once for two sweet eyes and a caressing accent. And next after this, the tongue is the great divider.

I am almost ashamed to pursue this worldly criticism of a religious rule; but there is yet another point in which the Trappist order appeals to me as a model of wisdom. By two in the morning the clapper goes upon the bell, and so on, hour by hour, and sometimes quarter by quarter, till eight, the hour of rest; so infinitesimally is the day divided among different occupations. The man who keeps rabbits, for example, hurries from his hutches to the chapel, the chapter-room, or the refectory, all day long: every hour he has an office to sing, a duty to perform; from two, when he rises in the dark, till eight, when he returns to receive the comfortable gift of sleep, he is upon his feet and occupied with manifold and changing business. I know many persons, worth several thousands in the year, who are not so fortunate in the disposal of their lives. Into how many houses would not the note of the monastery-bell, dividing the day into manageable portions, bring peace of mind and healthful activity of body?

We speak of hardships, but the true hardship is to be a dull fool, and permitted to mismanage life in our own dull and foolish manner.

From this point of view, we may perhaps better understand the monk's existence. A long novitiate, and every proof of constancy of mind and strength of body is required before admission to the order; but I could not find that many were discouraged. In the photographer's studio, which figures so strangely among the outbuildings, my eye was attracted by the portrait of a young fellow in the uniform of a private of foot. This was one of the novices, who came of the age for service, and marched and drilled and mounted guard for the proper time among the garrison of *Algiers*. Here was a man who had surely seen both sides of life before deciding; yet as soon as he was set free from service he returned to finish his novitiate.

This austere rule entitles a man to heaven as by right. When the Trappist sickens, he quits not his habit; he lies in the bed of death as he has prayed and labored in his frugal and silent existence; and when the Liberator comes, at the very moment, even before they have carried him in his robe to lie his little last in the chapel among continual chantings, joy-bells break forth, as if for a marriage, from the slated belfry, and proclaim throughout the neighborhood that another soul has gone to God.

At night, under the conduct of my kind Irishman, I took my place in the gallery to hear compline and *Salve Regina,* with which the Cistercians bring every day to a conclusion. There were none of those circumstances which strike the Protestant as childish or as tawdry in the public offices of *Rome*. A stern simplicity, heightened by the romance of the surroundings, spoke directly to the heart. I recall the white-washed chapel, the hooded figures in the choir, the lights alternately occluded and revealed, the strong manly singing, the silence that ensued, the sight of cowled heads bowed in prayer, and then the clear trenchant beating of the bell, breaking in to show that the last office was over and the hour of sleep had come; and when I remember, I am not surprised that I made my escape into the court with somewhat whirling fancies, and stood like a man bewildered in the windy starry night.

But I was weary; and when I had quieted my spirits with *Elizabeth Seton's* memoirs—a dull work—the cold and the raving of the wind among the pines—for my room was on that side of the monastery which adjoins the woods —disposed me readily to slumber. I was wakened at black midnight, as it seemed, though it was really two in the morning, by the first stroke upon the bell. All the brothers were then hurrying to the chapel; the dead in life, at this untimely hour, were already beginning the uncomforted labors of their day. The dead in life—there was a chill reflection. And the words of a French song came back into my memory, telling of the best of our mixed existence:—

> "Que t'as de belles filles,
> Giroflé!
> Girofla!
> Que t'as de belles filles,
> *L'Amour les comptera!*"

And I blessed God that I was free to wander, free to hope, and free to love.

THE BOARDERS

BUT there was another side to my residence at our *Lady of the Snows*. At this late season there were not many boarders; and yet I was not alone in the public part of the monastery. This itself is hard by the gate, with a small dining-room on the ground-floor, and a whole cor‑ridor of cells similar to mine up-stairs. I have stupidly forgotten the board for a regular *retraitant;* but it was somewhere between three and five francs a day, and I think most probably the first. Chance visitors like myself might give what they chose as a free-will offering, but nothing was demanded. I may mention that when I was going away, *Father Michael* refused twenty francs as ex‑cessive. I explained the reasoning which led me to offer him so much; but even then, from a curious point of honor, he would not accept it with his own hand. "I have no right to refuse for the monastery," he explained, "but I should prefer if you would give it to one of the brothers."

I had dined alone, because I arrived late; but at supper I found two other guests. One was a country parish priest, who had walked over that morning from the seat of his cure near *Mende* to enjoy four days of solitude and prayer. He was a grenadier in person, with the hale color and cir‑cular wrinkles of a peasant; and as he complained much of how he had been impeded by his skirts upon the march, I have a vivid fancy portrait of him, striding along, up‑right, big-boned, with kilted cassock, through the bleak hills of *Gévaudan*. The other was a short, grizzling, thick-set man, from forty-five to fifty, dressed in tweed with a knitted spencer, and the red ribbon of a decoration in his buttonhole. This last was a hard person to classify. He was an old soldier, who had seen service and risen to the rank of commandant; and he retained some of the brisk decisive manners of the camp. On the other hand, as soon as his resignation was accepted, he had come to our *Lady of the Snows* as a boarder, and, after a brief experience of its ways, had decided to remain as a novice. Already the new life was beginning to modify his appearance; already he had acquired somewhat of the quiet and smiling air of the brethren; and he was as yet neither an officer nor a Trappist, but partook of the character of each. And certainly here was a man in an interesting nick of life. Out of the noise of cannon and trumpets, he was in the act of passing into this still country bordering on the grave, where men sleep nightly in their grave-clothes, and, like phantoms, communicate by signs.

At supper we talked politics. I make it my business, when I am in *France,* to preach political good-will and moderation, and to dwell on the example of *Poland,* much as some alarmists in *England* dwell on the example of *Carthage*. The priest and the Commandant assured me of their sympathy with all I said, and made a heavy sighing over the bitterness of contemporary feeling.

"Why, you cannot say anything to a man with which he does not absolutely agree," said I, "but he flies up at you in a temper."

They both declared that such a state of things was anti-christian.

While we were thus agreeing, what should my tongue

stumble upon but a word in praise of *Gambetta's* moderation. The old soldier's countenance was instantly suffused with blood; with the palms of his hands he beat the table like a naughty child.

"*Comment, monsieur?*" he shouted. "*Comment? Gambetta* moderate? Will you dare to justify these words?"

But the priest had not forgotten the tenor of our talk. And suddenly, in the height of his fury, the old soldier found a warning look directed on his face; the absurdity of his behavior was brought home to him in a flash; and the storm came to an abrupt end, without another word.

It was only in the morning, over our coffee (*Friday, September 27th*), that this couple found out I was a heretic. I suppose I had misled them by some admiring expressions as to the monastic life around us; and it was only by a point-blank question that the truth came out. I had been tolerantly used, both by simple *Father Apollinaris* and astute *Father Michael;* and the good Irish deacon, when he heard of my religious weakness, had only patted me upon the shoulder and said, "You must be a Catholic and come to heaven." But I was now among a different sect of orthodox. These two men were bitter and upright and narrow, like the worst of Scotsmen, and indeed, upon my heart, I fancy they were worse. The priest snorted aloud like a battle-horse.

"*Et vous prétendez mourir dans cette espèce de croyance?*" he demanded; and there is no type used by mortal printers large enough to qualify his accent.

I humbly indicated that I had no design of changing.

But he could not away with such a monstrous attitude. "No, no," he cried; "you must change. You have come here, God has led you here, and you must embrace the opportunity."

I made a slip in policy; I appealed to the family affections, though I was speaking to a priest and a soldier, two classes of men circumstantially divorced from the kind and homely ties of life.

"Your father and mother?" cried the priest. "Very well; you will convert them in their turn when you go home."

I think I see my father's face! I would rather tackle the Gætulian lion in his den than embark on such an enterprise against the family theologian.

But now the hunt was up; priest and soldier were in full cry for my conversion; and the Work of the Propagation of the Faith, for which the people of *Cheylard* subscribed forty-eight francs ten centimes during 1877, was being gallantly pursued against myself. It was an odd but most effective proselytizing. They never sought to convince me in argument, where I might have attempted some defence; but took it for granted that I was both ashamed and terrified at my position, and urged me solely on the point of time. Now, they said, when God had led me to our *Lady of the Snows,* now was the appointed hour.

"Do not be withheld by false shame," observed the priest, for my encouragement.

For one who feels very similarly to all sects of religion, and who has never been able, even for a moment, to weigh seriously the merit of this or that creed on the eternal side of things, however much he may see to praise or blame upon the secular and temporal side, the situation thus created was both unfair and painful. I committed my second fault in tact, and tried to plead that it was all the same thing in the end, and we were all drawing near by different sides to that same kind and undiscriminating Friend and Father. That, as it seems to lay-spirits, would be the only gospel worthy of the name. But different men think differently; and this revolutionary aspiration brought down the priest with all the terrors of the law. He launched into harrowing details of hell. The damned, he said—on the authority of a little book which he had read not a week before, and which, to add conviction to conviction, he had fully intended to bring along with him in his pocket—were to occupy the same attitude through all eternity in the midst of dismal tortures. And as he thus expatiated, he grew in nobility of aspect with his enthusiasm.

As a result the pair concluded that I should seek out the Prior, since the Abbot was from home, and lay my case immediately before him.

"*C'est mon conseil comme ancien militaire,*" observed the Commandant; "*et celui de monsieur comme prêtre.*"

"*Oui,*" added the *curé*, sententiously nodding; "*comme ancien militaire—et comme prêtre.*"

At this moment, whilst I was somewhat embarrassed how to answer, in came one of the monks, a little brown fellow, as lively as a grig, and with an Italian accent, who threw himself at once into the contention, but in a milder and more persuasive vein, as befitted one of these pleasant brethren. Look at *him,* he said. The rule was very hard; he would have dearly liked to stay in his own country, *Italy*—it was well known how beautiful it was, the beautiful *Italy;* but then there were no Trappists in *Italy;* and he had a soul to save; and here he was.

I am afraid I must be at bottom, what a cheerful Indian critic has dubbed me, "a faddling hedonist"; for this description of the brother's motives gave me somewhat of a shock. I should have preferred to think he had chosen the life for its own sake, and not for ulterior purposes; and this shows how profoundly I was out of sympathy with these good Trappists, even when I was doing my best to sympathize. But to the *curé* the argument seemed decisive.

"Hear that!" he cried. "And I have seen a marquis here, a marquis, a marquis"—he repeated the holy word three times over—"and other persons high in society; and generals. And here, at your side, is this gentleman, who has been so many years in armies—decorated, an old warrior. And here he is, ready to dedicate himself to God."

I was by this time so thoroughly embarrassed that I pleaded cold feet, and made my escape from the apartment. It was a furious windy morning, with a sky much cleared, and long and potent intervals of sunshine; and I wandered until dinner in the wild country towards the east, sorely staggered and beaten upon by the gale, but rewarded with some striking views.

At dinner the Work of the Propagation of the Faith was recommenced, and on this occasion still more distastefully to me. The priest asked me many questions as to the contemptible faith of my fathers, and received my replies with a kind of ecclesiastical titter.

"Your sect," he said once; "for I think you will admit it would be doing it too much honor to call it a religion."

"As you please, monsieur," said I. "*La parole est à vous.*"

At length I grew annoyed beyond endurance; and although he was on his own ground, and, what is more to the purpose, an old man, and so holding a claim upon my toleration, I could not avoid a protest against his uncivil usage. He was sadly discountenanced.

"I assure you," he said, "I have no inclination to laugh in my heart. I have no other feeling but interest in your soul."

And there ended my conversion. Honest man! he was no dangerous deceiver; but a country parson, full of zeal and faith. Long may he tread *Gévaudan* with his kilted skirts—a man strong to walk and strong to comfort his parishioners in death! I dare say he would beat bravely through a snowstorm where his duty called him; and it is not always the most faithful believer who makes the cunningest apostle.

ACROSS THE GOULET

THE wind fell during dinner, and the sky remained clear, so it was under better auspices that I loalded *Modestine* before the monastery-gate. My Irish friend accompanied me so far on the way. As we came through the wood, there was *Père Apollinaire* hauling his barrow; and he too quitted his labors to go with me for perhaps a hundred yards, holding my hand between both of his in front of him. I parted first from one and then from the other with unfeigned regret, but yet with the glee of the traveller who shakes off the dust of one stage before hurrying forth upon another. Then *Modestine* and I mounted the course of the *Allier,* which here led us back into *Gévaudan* towards its sources in the forest of *Mercoire.* It was but an inconsiderable burn before we left its guidance. Thence, over a hill, our way lay through a naked plateau, until we reached *Chasseradès* at sundown.

The company in the inn-kitchen that night were all men employed in survey for one of the projected railways. They were intelligent and conversable, and we decided the future of *France* over hot wine, until the state of the clock frightened us to rest. There were four beds in the little up-stairs room; and we slept six. But I had a bed to myself, and persuaded them to leave the window open.

"Hé, bourgeois; il est cinq heures!" was the cry that wakened me in the morning (*Saturday, September* 28*th*). The room was full of a transparent darkness, which dimly

showed me the other three beds and the five different
night-caps on the pillows. But out of the window the
dawn was growing ruddy in a long belt over the hilltops,
and day was about to flood the plateau. The hour was
inspiriting; and there seemed a promise of calm weather,
which was perfectly fulfilled. I was soon under way with
Modestine. The road lay for a while over the plateau,
and then descended through a precipitous village into the
valley of the *Chassezac*. This stream ran among green
meadows, well hidden from the world by its steep banks;
the broom was in flower, and here and there was a hamlet
sending up its smoke.

At last the path crossed the *Chassezac* upon a bridge,
and, forsaking this deep hollow, set itself to cross the
mountain of *La Goulet*. It wound up through *Lestampes*
by upland fields and woods of beech and birch, and with
every corner brought me into an acquaintance with some
new interest. Even in the gully of the *Chassezac* my ear
had been struck by a noise like that of a great bass bell
ringing at the distance of many miles; but this, as I continued to mount and draw nearer to it, seemed to change
in character, and I found at length that it came from some
one leading flocks afield to the note of a rural horn. The
narrow street of *Lestampes* stood full of sheep, from wall
to wall—black sheep and white, bleating like the birds in
spring, and each one accompanying himself upon the
sheep-bell round his neck. It made a pathetic concert, all
in treble. A little higher, and I passed a pair of men in a
tree with pruning-hooks, and one of them was singing the
music of a *bourrée*. Still further, and when I was already
threading the birches, the crowing of cocks came cheerfully up to my ears, and along with that the voice of a

flute discoursing a deliberate and plaintive air from one of the upland villages. I pictured to myself some grizzled, apple-cheeked, country schoolmaster fluting in his bit of a garden in the clear autumn sunshine. All these beautiful and interesting sounds filled my heart with an unwonted expectation; and it appeared to me that, once past this range which I was mounting, I should descend into the garden of the world. Nor was I deceived, for I was now done with rains and winds and a bleak country. The first party of my journey ended here; and this was like an induction of sweet sounds into the other and more beautiful.

There are other degrees of *fey*ness, as of punishment, besides the capital; and I was now led by my good spirits into an adventure which I relate in the interest of future donkey-drivers. The road zigzagged so widely on the hillside that I chose a short cut by map and compass, and struck through the dwarf woods to catch the road again upon a higher level. It was my one serious conflict with *Modestine*. She would none of my short cut; she turned in my face, she backed, she reared; she, whom I had hitherto imagined to be dumb, actually brayed with a loud hoarse flourish, like a cock crowing for the dawn. I plied the goad with one hand; with the other, so steep was the ascent, I had to hold on the pack-saddle. Half a dozen times she was nearly over backwards on the top of me; half a dozen times, from sheer weariness of spirit, I was nearly giving it up, and leading her down again to follow the road. But I took the thing as a wager, and fought it through. I was surprised, as I went on my way again, by what appeared to be chill rain-drops falling on my hand, and more than once looked up in wonder at the cloudless sky. But it was only sweat which came dropping from my brow.

Over the summit of the *Goulet* there was no marked road—only upright stones posted from space to space to guide the drovers. The turf underfoot was springy and well scented. I had no company but a lark or two, and met but one bullock-cart between *Lestampes* and *Bleymard.* In front of me I saw a shallow valley, and beyond that the range of the *Lozère*, sparsely wooded and well enough modelled in the flanks, but straight and dull in outline. There was scarce a sign of culture; only about *Bleymard,* the white high-road from *Villefort* to *Mende* traversed a range of meadows, set with spiry poplars, and sounding from side to side with the bells of flocks and herds.

A NIGHT AMONG THE PINES

FROM *Bleymard* after dinner, although it was already late, I set out to scale a portion of the *Lozère*. An ill-marked stony drove-road guided me forward; and I met nearly half a dozen bullock-carts descending from the woods, each laden with a whole pine-tree for the winter's firing. At the top of the woods, which do not climb very high upon this cold ridge, I struck leftward by a path among the pines, until I hit on a dell of green turf, where a streamlet made a little spout over some stones to serve me for a water-tap. "In a more sacred or sequestered bower—nor nymph nor faunus haunted." The trees were not old, but they grew thickly round the glade: there was no outlook, except northeastward upon distant hill-tops, or straight upward to the sky; and the encampment felt secure and private like a room. By the time I had made my arrangements and fed *Modestine,* the day was already beginning to decline. I buckled myself to the knees into my sack and made a hearty meal; and as soon as the sun went down, I pulled my cap over my eyes and fell asleep.

Night is a dead monotonous period under a roof; but in the open world it passes lightly, with its stars and dews and perfumes, and the hours are marked by changes in the face of Nature. What seems a kind of temporal death to people choked between walls and curtains, is only a light and living slumber to the man who sleeps afield. All night long he can hear Nature breathing deeply and freely; even

as she takes her rest she turns and smiles; and there is one
stirring hour unknown to those who dwell in houses,
when a wakeful influence goes abroad over the sleeping
1emisphere, and all the out-door world are on their feet.
It is then that the cock first crows, not this time to announce the dawn, but like a cheerful watchman speeding
the course of night. Cattle awake on the meadows; sheep
break their fast on dewy hillsides, and change to a new
lair among the ferns; and houseless men, who have lain
down with the fowls, open their dim eyes and behold the
beauty of the night.

At what inaudible summons, at what gentle touch of
Nature, are all these sleepers thus recalled in the same
hour to life? Do the stars rain down an influence, or do
we share some thrill of mother earth below our resting
bodies? Even shepherds and old country-folk, who are the
deepest read in these arcana, have not a guess as to the
means or purpose of this nightly resurrection. Towards
two in the morning they declare the thing takes place; and
neither know nor inquire further. And at least it is a
pleasant incident. We are disturbed in our slumber only,
like the luxurious *Montaigne,* "that we may the better
and more sensibly relish it." We have a moment to look
upon the stars, and there is a special pleasure for some
minds in the reflection that we share the impulse with all
out-door creatures in our neighborhood, that we have escaped out of the *Bastille* of civilization, and are become,
for the time being, a mere kindly animal and a sheep of
Nature's flock.

When that hour came to me among the pines, I wakened thirsty. My tin was standing by me half full of
water. I emptied it at a draught; and feeling broad awake

after this internal cold aspersion, sat upright to make a cigarette. The stars were clear, colored, and jewel-like, but not frosty. A faint silvery vapor stood for the Milky Way. All around me the black fir-points stood upright and stock-still. By the whiteness of the pack-saddle, I could see *Modestine* walking round and round at the length of her tether; I could hear her steadily munching at the sward; but there was not another sound, save the indescribable quiet talk of the runnel over the stones. I lay lazily smoking and studying the color of the sky, as we call the void of space, from where it showed a reddish gray behind the pines to where it showed a glossy blue-black between the stars. As if to be more like a pedler, I wear a silver ring. This I could see faintly shining as I raised or lowered the cigarette; and at each whiff the inside of my hand was illuminated, and became for a second the highest light in the landscape.

A faint wind, more like a moving coolness than a stream of air, passed down the glade from time to time; so that even in my great chamber the air was being renewed all night long. I thought with horror of the inn at *Chasseradès* and the congregated nightcaps; with horror of the nocturnal prowesses of clerks and students, of hot theatres and pass-keys and close rooms. I have not often enjoyed a more serene possession of myself, nor felt more independent of material aids. The outer world, from which we cower into our houses, seemed after all a gentle habitable place; and night after night a man's bed, it seemed, was laid and waiting for him in the fields, where God keeps an open house. I thought I had rediscovered one of those truths which are revealed to savages and hid from political economists: at the least, I had discovered a new pleasure for myself. And yet even while I was exulting in my solitude I became aware of a strange lack. I wished a companion to lie near me in the starlight, silent and not moving, but ever within touch. For there is a fellowship more quiet even than solitude, and which, rightly understood, is solitude made perfect. And to live out of doors with the woman a man loves is of all lives the most complete and free.

As I thus lay, between content and longing, a faint noise stole towards me through the pines. I thought, at first, it was the crowing of cocks or the barking of dogs at some very distant farm; but steadily and gradually it took articulate shape in my ears, until I became aware that a passenger was going by upon the high-road in the valley, and singing loudly as he went. There was more of good-will than grace in his performance; but he trolled with ample lungs; and the sound of his voice took hold upon the hillside and set the air shaking in the leafy glens. I have heard people passing by night in sleeping cities; some of them sang; one, I remember, played loudly on the bagpipes. I have heard the rattle of a cart or carriage spring up suddenly after hours of stillness, and pass, for some minutes, within the range of my hearing as I lay abed. There is a romance about all who are abroad in the black hours, and with something of a thrill we try to guess their business. But here the romance was double: first, this glad passenger, lit internally with wine, who sent up his voice in music through the night; and then I, on the other hand, buckled into my sack, and smoking alone in the pine-woods between four and five thousand feet towards the stars.

When I awoke again (*Sunday, 29th September*), many

of the stars had disappeared; only the stronger companions of the the night still burned visibly overhead; and
away towards the east I saw a faint haze of light upon the
horizon, such as had been the Milky Way when I was last
awake. Day was at hand. I lit my lantern, and by its glow-
worm light put on my boots and gaiters; then I broke up
some bread for *Modestine,* filled my can at the water-tap,
and lit my spirit-lamp to boil myself some chocolate. The
blue darkness lay long in the glade where I had so sweetly
slumbered; but soon there was a broad streak of orange
melting into gold along the mountain-tops of *Vivarais.* A
solemn glee possessed my mind at this gradual and lovely
coming in of day. I heard the runnel with delight; I
looked round me for something beautiful and unexpect-
ed; but the still black pine-trees, the hollow glade, the
munching ass, remained unchanged in figure. Nothing
had altered but the light, and that, indeed, shed over all
a spirit of life and of breathing peace, and moved me to
a strange exhilaration.

I drank my water chocolate, which was hot if it was not
rich, and strolled here and there, and up and down about
the glade. While I was thus delaying, a gush of steady
wind, as long as a heavy sigh, poured direct out of the
quarter of the morning. It was cold, and set me sneezing.
The trees near at hand tossed their black plumes in its
passage; and I could see the thin distant spires of pine
along the edge of the hill rock slightly to and fro against
the golden east. Ten minutes after, the sunlight spread
at a gallop along the hillside, scattering shadows and
sparkles, and the day had come completely.

I hastened to prepare my pack, and tackle the steep
ascent that lay before me; but I had something on my

mind. It was only a fancy; yet a fancy will sometimes be importunate. I had been most hospitably received and punctually served in my green caravanserai. The room was airy, the water excellent, and the dawn had called me to a moment. I say nothing of the tapestries or the inimitable ceiling, nor yet of the view which I commanded from the windows; but I felt I was in some one's debt for all this liberal entertainment. And so it pleased me, in a half-laughing way, to leave pieces of money on the turf as I went along, until I had left enough for my night's lodging. I trust they did not fall to some rich and churlish drover.

THE COUNTRY OF THE CAMISARDS

"We travelled in the print of olden wars;
Yet all the land was green;
And love we found, and peace,
Where fire and war had been.
They pass and smile, the children of the sword—
No more the sword they wield;
And O, how deep the corn
Along the battle-field!"

W. P. BANNATYNE.

THE COUNTRY OF THE CAMISARDS

ACROSS THE LOZERE

THE track that I had followed in the evening soon
died out, and I continued to follow over a bald turf
ascent a row of stone pillars, such as had conducted me
across the *Goulet*. It was already warm. I tied my jacket
on the pack, and walked in my knitted waistcoat. *Modestine* herself was in high spirits, and broke of her own
accord, for the first time in my experience, into a jolting
trot that sent the oats swashing in the pocket of my coat.
The view, back upon the northern *Gévaudan,* extended
with every step; scarce a tree, scarce a house, appeared
upon the fields of wild hill that ran north, east, and west,
all blue and gold in the haze and sunlight of the morning. A multitude of little birds kept sweeping and twit-
tering about my path; they perched on the stone pillars,
they pecked and strutted on the turf, and I saw them
circle in volleys in the blue air, and show, from time to
time, translucent flickering wings between the sun and
me.

Almost from the first moment of my march, a faint
large noise, like a distant surf, had filled my ears. Sometimes I was tempted to think it the voice of a neighboring
waterfall, and sometimes a subjective result of the utter
stillness of the hill. But as I continued to advance, the
noise increased and became like the hissing of an enorm-

ous tea-urn, and at the same time breaths of cool air began to reach me from the direction of the summit. At length I understood. It was blowing stiffly from the south upon the other slope of the *Lozère,* and every step that I took I was drawing nearer to the wind.

Although it had been long desired, it was quite unexpectedly at last that my eyes rose above the summit. A step that seemed no way more decisive than many other steps that had preceded it—and, "like stout *Cortez* when, with eagle eyes, he stared on the *Pacific,*" I took possession, in my own name, of a new quarter of the world. For behold, instead of the gross turf rampart I had been mounting for so long, a view into the hazy air of heaven, and a land of intricate blue hills below my feet.

The *Lozère* lies nearly east and west, cutting *Gévaudan* into two unequal parts; its highest point, this *Pic de Finiels,* on which I was then standing, rises upwards of five thousand six hundred feet above the sea, and in clear weather commands a view over all lower *Languedoc* to the *Mediterranean Sea.* I have spoken with people who either pretended or believed that they had seen, from the *Pic de Finiels,* white ships sailing by *Montpellier* and *Cette.* Behind was the upland northern country through which my way had lain, peopled by a dull race, without wood, without much grandeur of hill-form, and famous in the past for little beside wolves. But in front of me, half-veiled in sunny haze, lay a new *Gévaudan,* rich picuresque, illustrious for stirring events. Speaking largely, I was in the *Cévennes* at *Monastier,* and during all my journey; but there is a strict and local sense in which only this confused and shaggy country at my feet has any title to the name, and in this sense the peasantry employ the word. These are the *Cévennes* with an emphasis: the *Cévennes* of the *Cévennes*. In that undecipherable labyrinth of hills, a war of bandits, a war of wild beasts, raged for two years between the Grand Monarch with all his troops and marshals on the one hand, and a few thousand Protestant mountaineers upon the other. A hundred and eighty years ago, the Camisards held a station even on the *Lozère*, where I stood; they had an organization, arsenals, a military and religious hierarchy; their affairs were "the discourse of every coffee-house" in *London; England* sent fleets in their support; their leaders prophesied and murdered; with colors and drums, and the singing of old French psalms, their bands sometimes affronted daylight, marched before walled cities, and dispersed the generals of the king; and sometimes at night, or in masquerade, possessed themselves of strong castles, and avenged treachery upon their allies and cruelty upon their foes. There, a hundred and eighty years ago, was the chivalrous *Roland, "Count* and *Lord Roland,* generalissimo of the Protestants in France," grave, silent, imperious, pockmarked ex-dragoon, whom a lady followed in his wanderings out of love. There was *Cavalier,* a baker's apprentice with a genius for war, elected brigadier of Comisards at seventeen, to die at fifty-five the English governor of *Jersey*. There again was *Castanet,* a partisan leader in a voluminous peruke and with a taste for controversial divinity. Strange generals, who moved apart to take counsel with the God of Hosts, and fled or offered battle, set sentinels or slept in an unguarded camp, as the Spirit whispered to their hearts! And there, to follow these and other leaders, was the rank and file of prophets and disciples, bold, patient, indefatigable, hardy to run upon the

mountains, cheering their rough life with psalms, eager
to fight, eager to pray, listening devoutly to the oracles
of brainsick children, and mystically putting a grain of
wheat among the pewter balls with which they charged
their muskets.

I had travelled hitherto through a dull district, and in
the track of nothing more notable than the child-eating
Beast of *Gévaudan*, the *Napoléon Buonaparte* of wolves.
But now I was to go down into the scene of a romantic
chapter—or, better, a romantic foot-note—in the history
of the world. What was left of all this bygone dust and
heroism? I was told that Protestantism still survived in
this head seat of Protestant resistance; so much the priest
himself had told me in the monastery parlor. But I had
yet to learn if it were a bare survival, or a lively and generous tradition. Again, if in the northern *Cévennes* the
people are narrow in religious judgments, and more filled
with zeal than charity, what was I to look for in this land
of persecution and reprisal—in a land where the tyranny
of the Church produced the Camisard rebellion, and the
terror of the Camisards threw the Catholic peasantry into
legalized revolt upon the other side, so that Camisard and
Florentin skulked for each other's lives among the mountains?

Just on the brow of the hill, where I paused to look
before me, the series of stone pillars came abruptly to an
end; and only a little below, a sort of track appeared and
began to go down a breakneck slope, turning like a cork-
screw as it went. It led into a valley between falling hills,
stubbly with rocks like a reaped field of corn, and floored
further down with green meadows. I followed the track
with precipitation; the steepness of the slope, the contin-

ual agile turning of the line of descent, and the old un-
wearied hope of finding something new in a new country,
all conspired to lend me wings. Yet a little lower and a
stream began, collecting itself together out of many fountains, and soon making a glad noise among the hills.
Sometimes it would cross the track in a bit of waterfall,
with a pool, in which *Modestine* refreshed her feet.

The whole descent is like a dream to me, so rapidly was
it accomplished. I had scarcely left the summit ere the
valley had closed round my path, and the sun beat upon
me, walking in a stagnant lowland atmosphere. The track
became a road, and went up and down in easy undula-
tions. I passed cabin after cabin, but all seemed deserted;
and I saw not a human creature, nor heard any sound except that of the stream. I was, however, in a different
country from the day before. The stony skeleton of the
world was here vigorously displayed to sun and air. The
slopes were steep and changeful. Oak-trees clung along
the hills, well grown, wealthy in leaf, and touched by the
autumn with strong and luminous colors. Here and there
another stream would fall in from the right or the left,
down a gorge of snow-white and tumultuary boulders.
The river in the bottom (for it was rapidly growing a
river, collecting on all hands as it trotted on its way) here
foamed awhile in desperate rapids, and there lay in pools
of the most enchanting sea-green shot with watery browns.
As far as I have gone, I have never seen a river of so
changeful and delicate a hue; crystal was not more clear,
the meadows were not by half so green; and at every pool
I saw I felt a thrill of longing to be out of these hot,
dusty, and material garments, and bathe my naked body
in the mountain air and water. All the time as I went on

J never forgot it was the Sabbath; the stillness was a per-petual reminder; and I heard in spirit the church-bells clamoring all over Europe, and the psalms of a thousand churches.

At length a human sound struck upon my ear—a cry strangely modulated between pathos and derision; and looking across the valley, I saw a little urchin sitting in a meadow, with his hands about his knees, and dwarfed to almost comical smallness by the distance. But the rogue had picked me out as I went down the road, from oak-wood on to oak-wood, driving *Modestine;* and he made me the compliments of the new country in this tremulous high-pitched salutation. And as all noises are lovely and natural at a sufficient distance, this also, coming through so much clean hill air and crossing all the green valley, sounded pleasant to my ear, and seemed a thing rustic, like the oaks or the river.

A little after, the stream that I was following fell into the *Tarn,* at *Pont de Montvert* of bloody memory.

PONT DE MONTVERT

ONE of the first things I encountered in *Pont de Montvert* was, if I remember rightly, the Protestant temple; but this was but the type of other novelties. A subtle atmosphere distinguishes a town in *England* from a town in *France,* or even in *Scotland.* At *Carlisle* you can see you are in one country; at *Dumfries,* thirty miles away, you are as sure that you are in the other. I should find it difficult to tell in what particulars *Pont de Montvert* differed from *Monastier* or *Langogne,* or even *Bleymard;* but the difference existed, and spoke eloquently to the eyes. The place, with its houses, its lanes, its glaring riverbed, wore an indescribable air of the South.

All was *Sunday* bustle in the streets and in the public-houses, as all had been Sabbath peace among the mountains. There must have been near a score of us at dinner by eleven before noon; and after I had eaten and drunken, and sat writing up my journal, I suppose as many more came dropping in one after another, or by twos and threes. In crossing the *Lozère* I had not only come among new natural features, but moved into the territory of a different race. These people, as they hurriedly despatched their viands in an intricate sword-play of knives, questioned and answered me with a degree of intelligence which excelled all that I had met, except among the railway folk at *Chasseradès.* They had open telling faces, and were lively both in speech and manner. They not only

entered thoroughly into the spirit of my little trip, but
more than one declared, if he were rich enough, he would
like to set forth on such another.

Even physically there was a pleasant change. I had not
seen a pretty woman since I left *Monastier,* and there but
one. Now of the three who sat down with me to dinner,
one was certainly not beautiful—a poor timid thing of
orty, quite troubled at this roaring *table d'hôte,* whom
I squired and helped to wine, and pledged and tried generally to encourage, with quite a contrary effect; but the
other two, both married, were both more handsome than
the average of women. And *Clarisse?* What shall I say of
Clarisse? She waited the table with a heavy placable non-
chalance, like a performing cow; her great gray eyes were
steeped in amorous languor; her features, although fleshy,
were of an original and accurate design; her mouth had a
curl; her nostril spoke of dainty pride; her cheek fell into
strange and interesting lines. It was a face capable of
strong emotion, and, with training, it offered the promise
of delicate sentiment. It seemed pitiful to see so good a
model left to country admirers and a country way of
thought. Beauty should at least have touched society;
then, in a moment, it throws off a weight that lay upon
it, it becomes conscious of itself, it puts on an elegance,
learns a gait and a carriage of the head, and, in a moment,
patet dea. Before I left I assured *Clarisse* of my hearty
admiration. She took it like milk, without embarrassment
or wonder, merely looking at me steadily with her great
eyes; and I own the result upon myself was some con-
fusion. If *Clarisse* could read English, I should not dare
to add that her figure was unworthy of her face. Hers was

a case for stays; but that may perhaps grow better as she gets up in years.

Pont de Montvert, or *Greenhill Bridge,* as we might say at home, is a place memorable in the story of the Camisards. It was here that the war broke out; here that those southern Covenanters slew their *Archbishop Sharpe.* The persecution on the one hand, the febrile enthusiasm on the other, are almost equally difficult to understand in these quiet modern days, and with our easy modern beliefs and disbeliefs. The Protestants were one and all beside their right minds with zeal and sorrow. They were all prophets and prophetesses. Children at the breast would exhort their parents to good works. "A child of fifteen months at *Quissac s*poke from its mother's arms, agitated and sobbing, distinctly and with a loud voice." *Marshall Villars* has seen a town where all the women "seemed possessed by the devil," and had trembling fits, and uttered prophecies publicly upon the streets. A prophetess of *Vivarais* was hanged at *Montpellier* because blood flowed from her eyes and nose, and she declared that she was weeping tears of blood for the misfortunes of the Protestants. And it was not only women and children. Stalwart dangerous fellows, used to swing the sickle or to wield the forest axe, were likewise shaken with strange paroxysms, and spoke oracles with sobs and streaming tears. A persecution unsurpassed in violence had lasted near a score of years, and this was the result upon the persecuted; hanging, burning, breaking on the wheel, had been vain; the dragoons had left their hoof-marks over all the country-side; there were men rowing in the galleys, and women pining in the prisons of the

Church; and not a thought was changed in the heart of any upright Protestant.

Now the head and forefront of the persecution—after *Lamoignon de Bavile*—*François de Langlade du Chayla* (pronounced *Chéïla*), Archpriest of the *Cévennes* and Inspector of Missions in the same country, had a house in which he sometimes dwelt in the town of *Pont de Montvert*. He was a conscientious person, who seems to have been intended by nature for a pirate, and now fifty-five, an age by which a man has learned all the moderation of which he is capable. A missionary in his youth in China, he there suffered martyrdom, was left for dead, and only succored and brought back to life by the charity of a pariah. We must suppose the pariah devoid of second sight, and not purposely malicious in this act. Such an experience, it might be thought, would have cured a man of the desire to persecute; but the human spirit is a thing strangely put together; and, having been a Christian martyr, *Du Chayla* became a Christian persecutor. The Work of the Propagation of the Faith went roundly forward in his hands. His house in *Pont de Montvert* served him as a prison. There he plucked out the hairs of the beard, and closed the hands of his prisoners upon live coals, to convince them that they were deceived in their opinions. And yet had not he himself tried and proved the inefficacy of these carnal arguments among the Boodhists in *China?*

Not only was life made intolerable in *Languedoc,* but flight was rigidly forbidden. One *Massip,* a muleteer, and well acquainted with the mountain-paths, had already guided several troops of fugitives in safety to *Geneva;* and on him, with another convoy, consisting mostly of women dressed as men, *Du Chayla,* in an evil hour for himself, laid his hands. The *Sunday* following, there was a conventicle of Protestants in the woods of *Altefage* upon *Mount Bougès;* where there stood up on *Séguier—Spirit Séguier,* as his companions called him—a wool-carder, tall, black-faced, and toothless, but a man full of prophecy. He declared, in the name of God, that the time for submission had gone by, and they must betake themselves to arms for the deliverance of their brethren and the destruction of the priests.

The next night, 24th *July,* 1702, a sound disturbed the Inspector of Missions as he sat in his prison-house at *Pont de Montvert;* the voices of many men upraised in psalmody drew nearer and nearer through the town. It was ten at night; he had his court about him, priests, soldiers, and servants, to the number of twelve or fifteen; and now dreading the insolence of a conventicle below his very windows, he ordered forth his soldiers to report. But the psalm-singers were already at his door, fifty strong, led by the inspired *Séguier,* and breathing death. To their summons, the archpriest made answer like a stout old persecutor, and bade his garrison fire upon the mob. One Camisard (for, according to some, it was in this night's work that they came by the name) fell at this discharge; his comrades burst in the door with hatchets and a beam of wood, overran the lower story of the house, set free the prisoners, and finding one of them in the *vine,* a sort of *Scavenger's Daughter* of the place and period, redoubled in fury against *Du Chayla,* and sought by repeated assaults to carry the upper floors. But he, on his side, had given absolution to his men, and they bravely held the staircase.

"Children of God," cried the prophet, "hold your

hands. Let us burn the house, with the priest and the
satellites of *Baal.*"

The fire caught readily. Out of an upper window *Du
Chayla* and his men lowered themselves into the garden
by means of knotted sheets; some escaped across the river
under the bullets of the insurgents; but the archpriest
himself fell, broke his thigh, and could only crawl into
the hedge. What were his reflections as this second martyrdom drew near? A poor, brave, besotted, hateful man,
who had done his duty resolutely according to his light
both in the *Cévennes* and *China*. He found at least one
telling word to say in his defence; for when the roof fell
in and the upbursting flames discovered his retreat, and
they came and dragged him to the public place of the
town, raging and calling him damned—"If I be damned,"
said he, "why should you also damn yourselves?"

Here was a good reason for the last; but in the course
of his inspectorship he had given many stronger which all
told in a contrary direction; and these he was now to
hear. One by one, *Séguier* first, the Camisards drew near
and stabbed him. "This," they said, "is for my father
broken on the wheel. This for my brother in the galleys.
That for my mother or my sister imprisoned in your cursed convents." Each gave his blow and his reason; and
then all kneeled and sang psalms around the body till the
dawn. With the dawn, still singing, they defiled away towards *Frugères,* further up the *Tarn,* to pursue the work
of vengeance, leaving *Du Chayla's* prison-house in ruins,
and his body pierced with two-and-fifty wounds upon the
public place.

'Tis a wild night's work, with its accompaniment of
psalms; and it seems as if a psalm must always have a

sound of threatening in that town upon the *Tarn.* But the story does not end, even so far as it concerns *Pont de Montvert,* with the departure of the Camisards. The career of *Séguier* was brief and bloody. Two more priests and a whole family at *Ladevèze,* from the father to the servants, fell by his hand or by his orders; and yet he was but a day or two at large, and restrained all the time by the presence of the soldiery. Taken at length by a famous soldier of fortune, *Captain Poul,* he appeared unmoved before his judges.

"Your name?" they asked.

"Pierre Séguier."

"Why are you called *Spirit?*"

"Because the Spirit of the Lord is with me."

"Your domicile?"

"Lately in the desert, and soon in heaven."

"Have you no remorse for your crimes?"

"I have committed none. *My soul is like a garden full of shelter and of fountains.*"

At *Pont de Montvert,* on the 12th of *August,* he had his right hand stricken from his body, and was burned alive. And his soul was like a garden? So perhaps was the soul of *Du Chayla,* the Christian martyr. And perhaps if you could read in my soul, or I could read in yours, our own composure might seem little less surprising.

Du Chayla's house still stands, with a new roof, beside one of the bridges of the town; and if you are curious you may see the terrace-garden into which he dropped.

IN THE VALLEY OF THE TARN

A NEW road leads from *Pont de Montvert* to *Florac* by
the valley of the *Tarn;* a smooth sandy ledge, it runs
about half-way between the summit of the cliffs and the
river in the bottom of the valley; and I went in and out,
as I followed it from bays of shadow into promontories of
afternoon sun. This was a pass like that of *Killiecrankie;*
a deep turning gully in the hills, with the *Tarn* making
a wonderful hoarse uproar far below, and craggy summits
standing in the sunshine high above. A thin fringe of
ash-trees ran about the hill-tops, like ivy on a ruin; but
on the lower slopes, and far up every glen the Spanish
chestnut-trees stood each four-square to heaven under its
tented foliage. Some were planted each on its own terrace, no larger than a bed; some, trusting in their roots,
found strength to grow and prosper and be straight and
large upon the rapid slopes of the valleys; others, where
there was a margin to the river, stood marshalled in a line
and mighty like the cedars of *Lebanon*. Yet even where
they grew most thickly they were not to be thought of as
a wood, but as a herd of stalwart individuals; and the
dome of each tree stood forth separate and large, and as
it were a little hill, from among the domes of its companions. They gave forth a faint sweet perfume which
pervaded the air of the afternoon; autumn had put tints
of gold and tarnish in the green; and the sun so shone
through and kindled the broad foliage, that each chestnut

was relieved against another, not in shadow, but in light.
A humble sketcher here laid down his pencil in despair.

I wish I could convey a notion of the growth of these
noble trees; of how they strike out boughs like the oak,
and trail sprays of drooping foliage like the willow; of
how they stand on upright fluted columns like the pillars
of a church; or like the olive, from the most shattered
bole can put out smooth and youthful shoots, and begin
a new life upon the ruins of the old. Thus they partake
of the nature of many different trees; and even their
prickly top-knots, seen near at hand against the sky, have
a certain palm-like air that impresses the imagination.
But their individuality, although compounded of so
many elements, is but the richer and the more original.
And to look down upon a level filled with these knolls of
foliage, or to see a clan of old unconquerable chestnuts
cluster "like herded elephants" upon the spur of a mountain, is to rise to higher thoughts of the powers that are
in Nature.

Between *Modestine's* laggard humour and the beauty
of the scene, we made little progress all that afternoon;
and at last finding the sun, although still far from setting,
was already beginning to desert the narrow valley of the
Tarn, I began to cast about for a place to camp in. This
was not easy to find; the terraces were too narrow, and
the ground, where it was unterraced, was usually too steep
for a man to lie upon. I should have slipped all night,
and awakened towards morning with my feet or my head
in the river.

After perhaps a mile, I saw, some sixty feet above the
road, a little plateau large enough to hold my sack, and
securely parapeted by the trunk of an aged and enormous

chestnut. Thither, with infinite trouble, I goaded and kicked the reluctant *Modestine,* and there I hastened to unload her. There was only room for myself upon the plateau, and I had to go nearly as high again before I found so much as standing room for the ass. It was on a heap of rolling stones, on an artificial terrace, certainly not five feet square in all. Here I tied her to a chestnut, and having given her corn and bread and made a pile of chestnut leaves, of which I found her greedy, I descended once more to my own encampment.

The position was unpleasantly exposed. One or two carts went by upon the road; and as long as daylight lasted I concealed myself, for all the world like a hunted Camisard, behind my fortification of vast chestnut trunk; for I was passionately afraid of discovery and the visit of jocular persons in the night. Moreover, I saw that I must be early awake; for these chestnut gardens had been the scene of industry no farther gone than on the day before. The slope was strewn with lopped branches, and here and there a great package of leaves was propped against a trunk; for even the leaves are serviceable, and the peasants use them in winter by way of fodder for their animals. I picked a meal in fear and trembling, half lying down to hide myself from the road; and I daresay I was as much concerned as if I had been a scout from *Joani's* band above the *Lozère* or from *Salmon's* across the *Tarn* in the old times of psalm-singing and blood. Or, indeed, perhaps more; for the Camisards had a remarkable confidence in God; and a tale comes back into my memory of how the *Count of Gévaudan,* riding with a party of dragoons and a notary at his saddlebow to enforce the oath of fidelity in all the country hamlets, entered a valley in the woods, and found *Cavalier* and his men at dinner, gayly seated on the grass, and their hats crowned with box-tree garlands, while fifteen women washed their linen in the stream. Such was a field festival in 1703; at that date *Antony Watteau* would be painting similar subjects.

This was a very different camp from that of the night before in the cool and silent pinewoods. It was warm and even stifling in the valley. The shrill song of frogs, like the tremolo note of a whistle with a pea in it, rang up from the riverside before the sun was down. In the growing dusk, faint rustlings began to run to and fro among the fallen leaves; from time to time a faint chirping or cheeping noise would fall upon my ear; and time to time I thought I could see the movement of something swift and indistinct between the chestnuts. A profusion of large ants swarmed upon the ground; bats whisked by, and mosquitos droned overhead. The long boughs with their bunches of leaves hung against the sky like garlands; and those immediately above and around me had somewhat the air of a trellis which should have been wrecked and half overthrown in a gale of wind.

Sleep for a long time fled my eyelids; and just as I was beginning to feel quiet stealing over my limbs, and settling densely on my mind, a noise at my head startled me broad awake again, and, I will frankly confess it, brought my heart into my mouth. It was such a noise as a person would make scratching loudly with a finger-nail, it came from under the knapsack which served me for a pillow, and it was thrice repeated before I had time to sit up and turn about. Nothing was to be seen, nothing more was to be heard, but a few of these mysterious rustlings far and near, and the ceaseless accompaniment of the river and the frogs. I learned next day that the chestnut gardens are infested by rats; rustling, chirping, and scraping were probably all due to these; but the puzzle, for the moment, was insoluble, and I had to compose myself for sleep, as best I could, in wondering uncertainty about my neighbours.

I was awakened in the gray of the morning (*Monday, 30th September*) by the sound of footsteps not far off upon the stones, and opening my eyes I beheld a peasant going by among the chestnuts by a footpath that I had not hitherto observed. He turned his head neither to the right nor to the left, and disappeared in a few strides among the foliage. Here was an escape! But it was plainly more than time to be moving. The peasantry were abroad; scarce less terrible to me in my nondescript position than the soldiers of *Captain Poul* to an undaunted Camisard. I fed *Modestine* with what haste I could; but as I was returning to my sack, I saw a man and a boy come down the hillside in a direction crossing mine. They unintelligibly hailed me, and I replied with inarticulate but cheerful sounds, and hurried forward to get into my gaiters.

The pair, who seemed to be father and son, came slowly up to the plateau, and stood close beside me for some time in silence. The bed was open, and I saw with regret my revolver lying patently disclosed on the blue wool. At last, after they had looked me all over, and the silence had grown laughably embarrassing, the man demanded in what seemed unfriendly tones:—

"You have slept here?"

"Yes," said I. "As you see."

"Why?" he asked.

"My faith," I answered lightly, "I was tired."

He next inquired where I was going and what I had had for dinner; and then, without the least transition, *"C'est bien,"* he added. "Come along." And he and his son, without another word, turned off to the next chestnut-tree but one, which they set to pruning. The thing had passed off more simply than I hoped. He was a grave, respectable man; and his unfriendly voice did not imply that he thought he was speaking to a criminal, but merely to an inferior.

I was soon on the road, nibbling a cake of chocolate and seriously occupied with a case of conscience. Was I to pay for my night's lodging? I had slept ill, the bed was full of fleas in the shape of ants, there was no water in the room, the very dawn had neglected to call me in the morning. I might have missed a train, had there been any in the neighborhood to catch. Clearly, I was dissatisfied with my entertainment; and I decided I should not pay unless I met a beggar.

The valley looked even lovelier by morning; and soon the road descended to the level of the river. Here, in a place where many straight and prosperous chestnuts stood together, making an aisle upon a swarded terrace, I made my morning toilette in the water of the *Tarn*. It was marvellously clear, thrillingly cool; the soap-suds disappeared as if by magic in the swift current, and the white boulders gave one a model for cleanliness. To wash in one of God's rivers in the open air seems to me a sort of cheerful solemnity or semi-pagan act of worship. To dabble among dishes in a bedroom may perhaps make clean the body; but the imagination takes no share in such a cleansing. I went on with a light and peaceful heart, and sang psalms to the spiritual ear as I advanced.

Suddenly up came an old woman, who point-blank demanded alms.

"Good!" thought I; "here comes the waiter with the bill."

And I paid for my night's lodging on the spot. Take it how you please, but this was the first and the last beggar that I met with during all my tour.

A step or two farther I was overtaken by an old man in a brown nightcap, clear-eyed, weather-beaten, with a faint, excited smile. A little girl followed him, driving two sheep and a goat; but she kept in our wake, while the old man walked beside me and talked about the morning and the valley. It was not much past six; and for healthy people who have slept enough, that is an hour of expansion and of open and trustful talk.

"Connaissez-vous le Seigneur?" he said at length.

I asked him what Seigneur he meant; but he only repeated the question with more emphasis and a look in his eyes denoting hope and interest.

"Ah!" said I, pointing upwards, "I understand you now. Yes, I know Him; He is the best of acquaintances."

The old man said he was delighted. "Hold," he added, striking his bosom; "it makes me happy here." There were a few who knew the Lord in these valleys, he went on to tell me; not many, but a few. "Many are called," he quoted, "and few chosen."

"My father," said I, "it is not easy to say who know the Lord; and it is none of our business. Protestants and Catholics, and even those who worship stones, may know Him and be known by Him; for He has made all."

I did not know I was so good a preacher.

The old man assured me he thought as I did, and repeated his expressions of pleasure at meeting me. "We are so few," he said. "They call us Moravians here; but down in the department of *Gard,* where there are also a good number, they are called Derbists, after an English pastor."

I began to understand that I was figuring, in questionable taste, as a member of some sect to me unknown; but I was more pleased with the pleasure of my companion than embarrassed by my own equivocal position. Indeed I can see no dishonesty in not avowing a difference; and especially in these high matters, where we have all a sufficient assurance that, whoever may be in the wrong, we ourselves are not completely in the right. The truth is much talked about; but this old man in a brown nightcap showed himself so simple, sweet, and friendly that I am not unwilling to profess myself his convert. He was, as a matter of fact, a Plymouth Brother. Of what that involves in the way of doctrine I have no idea nor the time to inform myself; but I know right well that we are all embarked upon a troublesome world, the children of one Father, striving in many essential points to do and to become the same. And although it was somewhat in a mistake that he shook hands with me so often and showed himself so ready to receive my words, that was a mistake of the truth-finding sort. For charity begins blindfold; and only through a series of similar misapprehensions rises at length into a settled principle of love and patience, and a firm belief in all our fellowmen. If I deceived this good old man, in the like manner I would willingly go on to deceive others. And if ever at length, out of our separate and sad ways, we should all come together into one common house, I have a hope, to which I cling dearly, that my mountain Plymouth Brother will hasten to shake hands with me again.

Thus, talking like *Christian* and *Faithful* by the way, he and I came down upon a hamlet by the *Tarn.* It was but a humble place, called *La Vernède,* with less than a dozen houses, and a Protestant chapel on a knoll. Here he dwelt; and here, at the inn, I ordered my breakfast. The inn was kept by an agreeable young man, a stone‑breaker on the road, and his sister, a pretty and engaging girl. The village school-master dropped in to speak with the stranger. And these were all Protestants—a fact which pleased me more than I should have expected; and, what pleased me still more, they seemed all upright and simple people. The Plymouth Brother hung around me with a sort of yearning interest, and returned at least thrice to make sure I was enjoying my meal. His behavior touched me deeply at the time, and even now moves me in recol- lection. He feared to intrude, but he would not willingly forego one moment of my society; and he seemed never weary of shaking me by the hand.

When all the rest had drifted off to their day's work, I sat for near half an hour with the young mistress of the house, who talked pleasantly over her seam of the chest- nut harvest, and the beauties of the *Tarn,* and old family affections, broken up when young folk go from home, yet still subsisting. Hers, I am sure, was a sweet nature, with a country plainness and much delicacy underneath; and he who takes her to his heart will doubtless be a fortun- ate young man.

The valley below *La Vernède* pleased me more and more as I went forward. Now the hills approached from either hand, naked and crumbling, and walled in the river between cliffs; and now the valley widened and became green. The road led me past the old castle of *Miral* on a steep; past a battlemented monastery, long since broken up and turned into a church and parsonage; and past a cluster of black roofs, the village of *Cocurès,* sitting among vineyards and meadows and orchards thick with red apples, and where, along the highway, they were knocking down walnuts from the roadside trees, and gathering them in sacks and baskets. The hills, however much the vale might open, were still tall and bare, with cliffy battlements and here and there a pointed summit; and the *Tarn* still rattled through the stones with a mountain noise. I had been led, by bagmen of a picturesque turn of mind, to expect a horrific country after the heart of *Byron;* but to my Scotch eyes it seemed smiling and plentiful, as the weather still gave an impression of high summer to my Scotch body; although the chestnuts were already picked out by the autumn, and the poplars, that here began to mingle with them, had turned into pale gold against the approach of winter.

There was something in this landscape, smiling although wild, that explained to me the spirit of the Southern Covenanters. Those who took to the hills for conscience' sake.

Scotland had all gloomy and bedevilled thoughts; for once that they received God's comfort they would be twice engaged with Satan; but the Camisards had only bright and supporting visions. They dealt much more in blood, both given and taken; yet I find no obsession of the Evil One in their records. With a light conscience, they pursued their life in these rough times and circumstances. The soul of *Séguier,* let us not forget, was like a garden. They knew they were on God's side, with a knowledge that has no parallel among the Scots; for the Scots, although they might be certain of the cause, could never rest confident of the person.

"We flew," says one old Camisard, "when we heard the sound of psalm-singing, we flew as if with wings. We felt within us an animating ardor, a transporting desire. The feeling cannot be expressed in words. It is a thing that must have been experienced to be understood. However weary we might be, we thought no more of our weariness and grew light, so soon as the psalms fell upon our ears."

The valley of the *Tarn* and the people whom I met at *La Vernède* not only explain to me this passage, but the twenty years of suffering which those, who were so stiff and so bloody when once they betook themselves to war, endured with the meekness of children and the constancy of saints and peasants.

FLORAC

O N a branch of the *Tarn* stands *Florac,* the seat of a subprefecture, with an old castle, an alley of planes, many quaint street-corners, and a live fountain welling from the hill. It is notable, besides, for handsome women, and as one of the two capitals, *Alais* being the other, of the country of the Camisards.

The landlord of the inn took me, after I had eaten, to an adjoining *café,* where I, or rather my journey, became the topic of the afternoon. Every one had some suggestion for my guidance; and the subprefectorial map was fetched from the subprefecture itself, and much thumbed among coffee-cups and glasses of liqueur. The most of these kind advisers were Protestant, though I observed that Protestant and Catholic intermingled in a very easy manner; and it surprised me to see what a lively memory still subsisted of the religious war. Among the hills of the south-west, by *Mauchline, Cummock,* or *Carsphairn,* in isolated farms or in the manse, serious Presbyterian people still recall the days of the great persecution, and the graves of local martyrs are still piously regarded. But in towns and among the so-called better classes, I fear that these old doings have become an idle tale. If you met a mixed company in the King's Arms at *Wigtown,* it is not likely that the talk would run on Covenanters. Nay, at *Muirkirk* of *Glenluce,* I found the beadle's wife had not so much as heard of *Prophet Peden.* But these Cévenols were proud of their ancestors in quite another sense; the war was their chosen topic; its exploits were their own patent of nobility; and where a man or a race has had but one adventure, and that heroic, we must expect and pardon some proxility of reference. They told me the country was still full of legends hitherto uncollected; I heard from them about *Cavalier's* descendants—not direct descendants, be it understood, but only cousins or nephews—who were still prosperous people in the scene of the boy-general's exploits; and one farmer had seen the bones of old combatants dug up into the air of an afternoon in the nineteenth century, in a field where the ancestors had fought, and the great-grandchildren were peaceably ditching.

Later in the day one of the Protestant pastors was so good as to visit me: a young man, intelligent and polite, with whom I passed an hour or two in talk. *Florac,* he told me, is part Protestant, part Catholic; and the difference in religion is usually doubled by a difference in politics. You may judge of my surprise, coming as I did from such a babbling purgatorial *Poland* of a place as *Monastier,* when I learned that the population lived together on very quiet terms; and there was even an exchange of hospitalities between households thus doubly separated. Black Camisard and White Camisard, militiaman and Miquelet and dragoon, Protestant prophet and Catholic cadet of the White Cross, they had all been sabring and shooting, burning, pillaging and murdering, their hearts hot with indignant passion; and here, after a hundred and seventy years, Protestant is still Protestant, Catholic still Catholic, in mutual toleration and mild amity of life. But the race of man, like that indomitable nature whence it sprang, has medicating virtues of its own; the years and seasons bring various harvests; the sun returns after the rain; and mankind outlives secular animosities, as a single man awakens from the passions of a day. We judge our ancestors from a more divine position; and the dust being a little laid with several centuries, we can see both sides adorned with human virtues and fighting with a show of right.

I have never thought it easy to be just, and find it daily even harder than I thought. I own I met these Protestants with delight and a sense of coming home. I was accustomed to speak their language, in another and deeper sense of the word than that which distinguishes between French and English; for the true babel is a divergence upon morals. And hence I could hold more free communication with the Protestants, and judge them more justly, than the Catholics. *Father Apollinaris* may pair off with my mountain Plymouth Brother as two guileless and devout old men; yet I ask myself if I had as ready a feeling for the virtues of the Trappist; or had I been a Catholic, if I should have felt so warmly to the dissenter of *La Vernède*. With the first I was on terms of mere forbearance; but with the other, although only on a misunderstanding and by keeping on selected points, it was still possible to hold converse and exchange some honest thoughts. In this world of imperfection we gladly welcome even partial intimacies. If we find but one to whom we can speak out of our heart freely, with whom we can walk in love and simplicity with out dissimulation, we have no ground of quarrel with the world or God.

IN THE VALLEY OF THE MIMENTE

O N *Tuesday, 1st October,* we left *Florac* late in the
afternoon, a tired donkey and tired donkey-driver.
A little way up the *Tarnon,* a covered bridge of wood introduced us into the valley of the *Mimente.* Steep rocky
red mountains overhung the stream; great oaks and chestnuts grew upon the slopes or in stony terraces; here and
there was a red field of millet or a few apple-trees studded
with red apples; and the road passed hard by two black
hamlets, one with an old castle atop to please the heart
of the tourist.

It was difficult here again to find a spot fit for my encampment. Even under the oaks and chestnuts the
ground had not only a very rapid slope, but was heaped
with loose stones; and where there was no timber the hills
descended to the stream in a red precipice tufted with
heather. The sun had left the highest peak in front of
me, and the valley was full of the lowing sound of herds-
men's horns as they recalled the flocks into the stable,
when I spied a bight of meadow some way below the roadway in an angle of the river. Thither I descended, and,
tying *Modestine* provisionally to a tree, proceeded to in-
vestigate the neighborhood. A gray pearly evening shadow filled the glen; objects at a little distance grew indistinct and melted bafflingly into each other; and the
darkness was rising steadily like an exhalation. I approached a great oak which grew in the meadow, hard by

the river's brink; when to my disgust the voices of children fell upon my ear, and I beheld a house round the angle on the other bank. I had half a mind to pack and be gone again, but the growing darkness moved me to remain. I had only to make no noise until the night was fairly come, and trust to the dawn to call me early in the morning. But it was hard to be annoyed by neighbors in such a great hotel.

A hollow underneath the oak was my bed. Before I had fed *Modestine* and arranged my sack, three stars were already brightly shining, and the others were beginning dimly to appear. I slipped down to the river, which looked very black among its rocks, to fill my can; and dined with a good appetite in the dark, for I scrupled to light a lantern while so near a house. The moon, which I had seen, a pallid crescent, all afternoon, faintly illuminated the summit of the hills, but not a ray fell into the bottom of the glen where I was lying. The oak rose before me like a pillar of darkness; and overhead the heartsome stars were set in the face of the night. No one knows the stars who has not slept, as the French happily put it, *à la belle étoile*. He may know all their names and distances and magnitudes, and yet be ignorant of what alone concerns mankind, their serene and gladsome influence on the mind. The greater part of poetry is about the stars; and very justly, for they are themselves the most classical of poets. These same far-away worlds, sprinkled like tapers or shaken together like a diamond dust upon the sky, had looked not otherwise to *Roland* or *Cavalier,* when, in the words of the latter, they had "no other tent but the sky, and no other bed than my mother earth."

All night a strong wind blew up the valley, and the

acorns fell pattering over me from the oak. Yet, on this first night of *October,* the air was as mild as *May,* and I slept with the fur thrown back.

I was much disturbed by the barking of a dog, an animal that I fear more than any wolf. A dog is vastly braver, and is besides supported by the sense of duty. If you kill a wolf, you meet with encouragement and praise; but if you kill a dog, the sacred rights of property and the domestic affections come clamoring round you for redress. At the end of a fagging day, the sharp, cruel note of a dog's bark is in itself a keen annoyance; and to a tramp like myself, he represents the sedentary and respectable world in its most hostile form. There is something of the clergyman or the lawyer about this engaging animal; and if he were not amenable to stones, the boldest man would shrink from travelling afoot. I respect dogs much in the domestic circle; but on the highway or sleeping afield, I both detest and fear them.

I was awakened next morning (*Wednesday, October 2d*) by the same dog—for I knew his bark—making a charge down the bank, and then, seeing me sit up, retreating again with great alacrity. The stars were not yet quite extinguished. The heaven was of that enchanting mild gray-blue of the early morn. A still clear light began to fall, and the trees on the hillside were outlined sharply against the sky. The wind had veered more to the north, and no longer reached me in the glen; but as I was going on with my preparations, it drove a white cloud very swiftly over the hill-top; and looking up, I was surprised to see the cloud dyed with gold. In these high regions of the air, the sun was already shining as at noon. If only the clouds travelled high enough, we should see the same thing all night long.   For it is always daylight in the fields of space.

As I began to go up the valley, a draught of wind came down it out of the seat of the sunrise, although the clouds continued to run overhead in an almost contrary direction. A few steps farther, and I saw a whole hillside gilded with the sun; and still a little beyond, between two peaks, a centre of dazzling brilliancy appeared floating in the sky, and I was once more face to face with the big bonfire that occupies the kernel of our system.

I met but one human being that forenoon, a dark military-looking wayfarer, who carried a game-bag on a baldric; but he made a remark that seems worthy of record.   For when I asked him if he were Protestant or Catholic—

"O," said he, "I make no shame of my religion.   I am a Catholic."

He made no shame of it!   The phrase is a piece of natural statistics; for it is the language of one in a minority.   I thought with a smile of *Bavile* and his dragoons, and how you may ride rough-shod over a religion for a century, and leave it only the more lively for the friction. *Ireland* is still Catholic; the *Cévennes* still Protestant.   It is not a basketful of law-papers, nor the hoofs and pistol-butts of a regiment of horse, that can change one tittle of a ploughman's thoughts.   Outdoor rustic people have not many ideas, but such as they have are hardy plants and thrive flourishingly in persecution.   One who has grown a long while in the sweat of laborious noons, and under the stars at night, a frequenter of hills and forests, an old honest countryman, has, in the end, a sense of communion with the powers of the universe, and amicable relations towards his God. Like my mountain Plymouth Brother, he knows the Lord. His religion does not repose upon a choice of logic; it is the poetry of the man's experience, the philosophy of the history of his life. God, like a great power, like a great shining sun, has appeared to this simple fellow in the course of years, and become the ground and essence of his least reflections; and you may change creeds and dogmas by authority, or proclaim a new religion with the sound of trumpets, if you will; but here is a man who has his own thoughts, and will stubbornly adhere to them in good and evil. He is a Catholic, a Protestant, or a Plymouth Brother, in the same indefeasible sense that a man is not a woman, or a woman not a man. For he could not vary from his faith, unless he could eradicate all memory of the past, and, in a strict and not a conventional meaning, change his mind.

THE HEART OF THE COUNTRY

I WAS now drawing near to *Cassagnas,* a cluster of black roofs upon the hillside, in this wild valley, among chestnut gardens, and looked upon in the clear air by many rocky peaks. The road along the *Mimente* is yet new, nor have the mountaineers recovered their surprise when the first cart arrived at *Cassagnas.* But although it lay thus apart from the current of men's business, this hamlet had already made a figure in the history of *France.* Hard by, in caverns of the mountain, was one of the five arsenals of the Camisards; where they laid up clothes and corn and arms against necessity, forged bayonets and sabers, and made themselves gunpowder with willow charcoal and saltpetre boiled in kettles. To the same caves, amid this multifarious industry, the sick and wounded were brought up to heal; and there they were visited by the two surgeons, *Chabrier* and *Tavan,* and secretly nursed by women of the neighborhood.

Of the five legions into which the Camisards were divided, it was the oldest and the most obscure that had its magazines by *Cassagnas.* This was the band of *Spirit Séguier;* men who had joined their voices with his in the 68th Psalm as they marched down by night on the archpriest of the *Cévennes, Séguier,* promoted to heaven, was succeeded by *Salomon Couderc,* whom *Cavalier* treats in his memoirs as chaplain-general to the whole army of the Camisards. He was a prophet; a great reader of the heart, who admitted people to the sacrament or refused them by "intentively viewing every man" between the eyes; and had the most of the Scriptures off by rote. And this was surely happy; since in a surprise in August, 1703, he lost his mule, his portfolios, and his Bible. It is only strange that they were not surprised more often and more effectually; for this legion of *Cassagnas* was truly patriarchal in its theory of war, and camped without sentries, leaving that duty to the angels of the God for whom they fought. This is a token, not only of their faith, but of the trackless country where they harbored. *M. de Caladon,* taking a stroll one fine day, walked without warning into their midst, as he might have walked into "a flock of sheep in a plain," and found some asleep and some awake and psalm-singing. A traitor had need of no recommendation to insinuate himself among their ranks, beyond "his faculty of singing psalms"; and even the prophet *Salomon* "took him into a particular friendship." Thus, among their intricate hills, the rustic troop subsisted; and history can attribute few exploits to them but sacraments and ecstasies.

People of this tough and simple stock will not, as I have just been saying, prove variable in religion; nor will they get nearer to apostasy than a mere external conformity like that of *Naaman* in the house of *Rimmon.* When *Louis XVI.,* in the words of the edict, "convinced by the uselessness of a century of persecutions, and rather from necessity than sympathy," granted at last a royal grace of toleration, *Cassagnas* was still Protestant; and to a man, it is so to this day. There is, indeed, one family that is not Protestant, but neither is it Catholic. It is that of a Catholic *curé* in revolt, who has taken to his bosom a schoolmis-

tress. And his conduct, it's worth noting, is disapproved
by the Protestant villagers.

"It is a bad idea for a man," said one, "to go back from
his engagements."

The villagers whom I saw seemed intelligent after a
countrified fashion, and were all plain and dignified in
manner. As a Protestant myself, I was well looked upon,
and my acquaintance with history gained me farther respect. For we had something not unlike a religious con
troversy at table, a gendarme and a merchant with whom
I dined being both strangers to the place and Catholics.
The young men of the house stood round and supported
me; and the whole discussion was tolerantly conducted,
and surprised a man brought up among the infinitesimal
and contentious differences of Scotland. The merchant,
indeed, grew a little warm, and was far less pleased than
some others with my historical acquirements. But the
gendarme was mighty easy over it all.

"It's a bad idea for a man to change," said he; and the
remark was generally applauded.

That was not the opinion of the priest and soldier at
our *Lady of the Snows.* But this is a different race; and
perhaps the same great-heartedness that upheld them to
resist, now enables them to differ in a kind spirit. For
courage respects courage; but where a faith has been trod-
den out, we may look for a mean and narrow population.
The true work of *Bruce* and *Wallace* was the union of the
nations; not that they should stand apart a while longer,
skirmishing upon their borders; but that, when the time
came, they might unite with self-respect.

The merchant was much interested in my journey, and
thought it dangerous to sleep afield.

"There are the wolves," said he; "and then it is known you are an Englishman. The English have always long purses, and it might very well enter into some one's head to deal you an ill blow some night."

I told him I was not much afraid of such accidents; and at any rate judged it unwise to dwell upon alarms or consider small perils in the arrangement of life. Life itself, I submitted, was a far too risky business as a whole to make each additional particular of danger worth regard. "Something," said I, "might burst in your inside any day of the week, and there would be an end of you, if you were locked into your room with three turns of the key."

"*Cependant,*" said he, "*coucher dehors!*"

"God," said I, "is everywhere."

"*Cependant, coucher dehors!*" he repeated, and his voice was eloquent of terror.

He was the only person, in all my voyage, who saw anything hardy in so simple a proceeding; although many considered it superfluous. Only one, on the other hand, professed much delight in the idea; and that was my Plymouth Brother, who cried out, when I told him I sometimes preferred sleeping under the stars to a close and noisy alehouse, "Now I see that you know the Lord!"

The merchant asked me for one of my cards as I was leaving for he said I should be something to talk of in the future, and desired me to make a note of his request and reason; a desire with which I have thus complied.

A little after two I struck across the *Mimente,* and took a rugged path southward up a hillside covered with loose stones and tufts of heather. At the top, as in the habit of the country, the path disappeared; and I left my she-ass munching heather, and went forward alone to seek a road.

I was now on the separation of two vast watersheds; behind me all the streams were bound for the *Garonne* and
the Western Ocean; before me was the basin of the
Rhone. Hence, as from the *Lozère*, you can see in clear
weather the shining of the *Gulf of Lyons;* and perhaps
from here the soldiers of *Salomon* may have watched for
the topsails of *Sir Cloudesley Shovel*, and the long-promis-
ed aid from *England*. You may take this ridge as lying in
the heart of the country of the Camisards; four of the
five legions camped all round it and almost within view—
Salomon and *Joani* to the north, *Castanet* and *Roland* to
the south; and when *Julien* had finished his famous work,
the devastation of the *High Cévennes*, which lasted all
through *October* and *November*, 1703, and during which
four hundred and sixty villages and hamlets were, with
fire and pickaxe, utterly subverted, a man standing on
this eminence would have looked forth upon a silent,
smokeless, and dispeopled land. Time and man's activity
have now repaired these ruins; *Cassagnas* is once more
roofed and sending up domestic smoke; and in the chestnut gardens, in low and leafy corners, many a prosperous
farmer returns, when the day's work is done, to his children and bright hearth. And still it was perhaps the wildest
view of all my journey. Peak upon peak, chain upon
chain of hills ran surging southward, channelled and
sculptured by the winter streams, feathered from head to
foot with chestnuts, and here and there breaking out into
a coronal of cliffs. The sun, which was still far from
setting, sent a drift of misty gold across the hilltops, but
the valleys were already plunged in a profound and quiet
shadow.

A very old shepherd, hobbling on a pair of sticks, and

wearing a black cap of liberty, as if in honor of his near-
ness to the grave, directed me to the road for *St. Germain
de Calberte*. There was something solemn in the isolation
of this infirm and ancient creature. Where he dwelt, how
he got upon this high ridge, or how he proposed to get
down again, were more than I could fancy. Not far off
upon my right was the famous *Plan de Font Morte*, where
Poul with his Armenian sabre slashed down the Camisards of *Séguier*. This, methought, might be some *Rip
van Winkle* of the war, who had lost his comrades, fleeing
before *Poul,* and wandered ever since upon the mountains. It might be news to him that *Cavalier* had surrend-
ered, or *Roland* had fallen fighting with his back against
an olive. And while I was thus working on my fancy, I
heard him hailing in broken tones, and saw him waving
me to come back with one of his two sticks. I had already
got some way past him; but, leaving *Modestine* once more,
retraced my steps.

Alas, it was a very commonplace affair. The old gen-
teman had forgot to ask the pedler what he sold, and wished to remedy this neglect.

I told him sternly, "Nothing."

"Nothing?" cried he.

I repeated "Nothing," and made off.

It's odd to think of, but perhaps I thus became as inexplicable to the old man as he had been to me.

The road lay under chestnuts, and though I saw a hamlet or two below me in the vale, and many lone houses
of the chestnut farmers, it was a very solitary march all
afternoon; and the evening began early underneath the
trees. But I heard the voice of a woman singing some sad,
old, endless ballad not far off. It seemed to be about love

and a *bel amoureux,* her handsome sweetheart; and I wished I could have taken up the strain and answered her, as I went on upon my invisible woodland way, weaving, like *Pippa* in the poem, my own thoughts with hers. What could I have told her? Little enough; and yet all the heart requires. How the world gives and takes away, and brings sweethearts near, only to separate them again into distant and strange lands; but to love is the great amulet which makes the world a garden; and "hope, which comes to all," outwears the accidents of life, and reaches with tremulous hand beyond the grave and death. Easy to say: yea, but also, by God's mercy, both easy and grateful to believe!

We struck at last into a wide white high-road, carpeted with noiseless dust. The night had come; the moon had been shining for a long while upon the opposite mountain; when on turning a corner my donkey and I issued ourselves into her light. I had emptied out my brandy at *Florac,* for I could bear the stuff no longer, and replaced it with some generous and scented Volnay; and now I drank to the moon's sacred majesty upon the road. It was but a couple of mouthfuls; yet, I became thenceforth unconscious of my limbs, and my blood flowed with luxury. Even *Modestine* was inspired by this purified nocturnal sunshine, and bestirred her little hoofs as to a livelier measure. The road wound and descended swiftly among masses of chestnuts. Hot dust rose from our feet and flowed away. Our two shadows—mine deformed with the knapsack, hers comically bestridden by the pack—now lay before us clearly outlined on the road, and now, as we turned a corner, went off into the ghostly distance, and sailed along the mountainlike clouds. From time to time

a warm wind rustled down the valley, and set all the chestnuts dangling their bunches of foliage and fruit; the ear
was filled with whispering music, and the shadows danced
in tune. And next moment the breeze had gone by, and
in all the valley nothing moved except our travelling feet.
On the opposite slope, the monstrous ribs and gullies of
the mountain were faintly designed in the moonshine;
and high overhead, in some lone house, there burned one
lighted window, one square spark of red in the huge field
of sad nocturnal coloring.

At a certain point, as I went downward, turning many
acute angles, the moon disappeared behind the hill; and I
pursued my way in great darkness, until another turning
shot me without preparation into *St. Germain de Calberte.*
The place was asleep and silent, and buried in opaque
night. Only from a single open door, some lamplight
escaped upon the road to show me I was come among
men's habitations. The two last gossips of the evening,
still talking by a garden wall, directed me to the inn. The
landlady was getting her chicks to bed; the fire was already
out, and had, not without grumbling, to be rekindled;
half an hour later, and I must have gone supperless to
roost.

THE LAST DAY

W HEN I awoke (*Thursday, 2nd October*), and, hearing a great flourishing of cocks and chuckling of
contented hens, betook me to the window of the clean and
comfortable room where I had slept the night, I looked
forth on a sunshiny morning in a deep vale of chestnut gardens. It was still early, and the cockcrows, and the slant-
ing lights, and the long shadows encouraged me to be out
and look round me.

St. Germain de Calberte is a great parish nine leagues
round about. At the period of the wars, and immediately
before the devastation, it was inhabited by two hundred
and seventy-five families, of which only nine were Catholic; and it took the *curé* seventeen *September* days to go
from house to house on horseback for a census. But the
place itself, although capital of a canton, is scarce larger
than a hamlet. It lies terraced across a steep slope in the
midst of mighty chestnuts. The Protestant chapel stands
below upon a shoulder; in the midst of the town is the
quaint old Catholic church.

It was here that poor *Du Chayla,* the Christian martyr,
kept his library and held a court of missionaries; here he
had built his tomb, thinking to lie among a grateful population whom he had redeemed from error; and hither on
the morrow of his death they brought the body, pierced
with two-and-fifty wounds, to be interred. Clad in his
priestly robes, he was laid out in state in the church. The

curé, taking his text from Second Samuel, twentieth chapter and twelfth verse, "And *Amasa* wallowed in his blood in the highway," preached a rousing sermon, and exhorted his brethren to die each at his post, like their unhappy and illustrious superior. In the midst of this eloquence there came a breeze that *Spirit Séguier* was near at hand; and behold! all the assembly took to their horses' heels, some east, some west, and the *curé* himself as far as *Alais.*

Strange was the position of this little Catholic metropolis, a thimbleful of *Rome,* in such a wild and contrary neighborhood. On the one hand, the legion of *Salomon* overlooked it from *Cassagnas;* on the other, it was cut off from assistance by the legion of *Roland* at *Mialet.* The *curé, Louvrelenil,* although he took a panic at the archpriest's funeral, and so hurriedly decamped to *Alais,* stood well by his isolated pulpit, and hence uttered fulminations against the crimes of the Protestants. *Salomon* besieged the village for an hour and a half, but was beat back. The militiamen, on guard before the *curé's* door, could be heard, in the black hours, singing Protestant psalms and holding friendly talk with the insurgents. And in the morning, although not a shot had been fired, there would not be a round of powder in their flasks. Where was it gone? All handed over to the Camisards for a consideration. Untrusty guardians for an isolated priest!

That these continual stirs were once busy in *St. Germain de Calberte,* the imagination with difficulty receives; all is now so quiet, the pulse of human life nows beats so low and still in this hamlet of the mountains. Boys followed me a great way off, like a timid sort of lion-hunters; and people turned round to have a second look, or came out of their houses, as I went by. My passage was the first event, you would have fancied, since the Camisards. There was nothing rude or forward in this observation; it was but a pleased and wondering scrutiny, like that of oxen or the human infant; yet it wearied my spirits, and soon drove me from the street.

I took refuge on the terraces, which are here greenly carpeted with sward, and tried to imitate with a pencil the inimitable attitudes of the chestnuts as they bear up their canopy of leaves. Ever and again a little wind went by, and the nuts dropped all around me, with a light and dull sound, upon the sward. The noise was as of a thin fall of great hailstones; but there went with it a cheerful human sentiment of an approaching harvest and farmers rejoicing in their gains. Looking up, I could see the brown nut peering through the husk, which was already gaping; and between the stems the eye embraced an amphitheatre of hill, sunlit and green with leaves.

I have not often enjoyed a place more deeply. I moved in an atmosphere of pleasure, and felt light and quiet and content. But perhaps it was not the place alone that so disposed my spirit. Perhaps some one was thinking of me in another country; or perhaps some thought of my own had come and gone unnoticed, and yet done me good. For some thoughts, which sure would be the most beautiful, vanish before we can rightly scan their features; as though a god, travelling by our green highways, should but ope the door, give one smiling look into the house, and go again forever. Was it *Apollo,* or *Mercury,* or Love with folded wings? Who shall say? But we go the lighter about our business, and feel peace and pleasure in our hearts.

I dined with a pair of Catholics. They agreed in the condemnation of a young man, a Catholic, who had married a Protestant girl and gone over to the religion of his wife. A Protestant born they could understand and respect; indeed, they seemed to be of the mind of an old Catholic woman, who told me that same day there was no difference between the two sects, save that "wrong was more wrong for the Catholic," who had more light and guidance; but this of a man's desertion filled them with contempt.

"It is a bad idea for a man to change," said one.

It may have been accidental, but you see how this phrase pursued me; and for myself, I believe it is the current philosophy in these parts. I have some difficulty in imagining a better. It's not only a great flight of confidence for a man to change his creed and go out of his family for heaven's sake; but the odds are—nay, and the hope is—that, with all this great transition in the eyes of man, he has not changed himself a hair's breadth to the eyes of God. Honor to those who do so, for the wrench is sore. But it argues something narrow, whether of strength or weakness, whether of the prophet or the fool, in those who can take a sufficient interest in such infinitesimal and human operations, or who can quit a friendship for a double process of the mind. And I think I should not leave my old creed for another, changing only words for other words; but by some brave reading, embrace it in spirit and truth, and find wrong as wrong for me as for the best of other communions.

The *phylloxera* was in the neighborhood; and instead of wine we drank at our dinner a more economical juice of the grape—*la Parisienne,* they call it. It is made by putting the fruit whole into a cask with water; one by one the berries ferment and burst; what is drunk during the day is supplied at night in water; so, with ever another pitcher from the well, and ever another grape exploding and giving out its strength, one cask of *Parisienne* may last a family till spring. It is, as the reader will anticipate, a feeble beverage, but very pleasant to the taste.

What with dinner and coffee, it was long past three before I left *St. Germain de Calberte*. I went down beside the *Gardon of Mialet,* a great glaring watercourse devoid of water, and through *St. Etienne de Vallée Française,* or *Val Francesque,* as they used to call it; and towards evening began to ascend the hill of *St. Pierre.* It was a long and steep ascent. Behind me an empty carriage returning to *St. Jean du Gard* kept hard upon my tracks, and near the summit overtook me. The driver, like the rest of the world, was sure I was a pedler; but, unlike others, he was sure of what I had to sell. He had noticed the blue wool which hung out of my pack at either end; and from this he had decided, beyond my power to alter his decision, that I dealt in blue-wool collars, such as decorate the neck of the French draught-horse.

I had hurried to the topmost powers of *Modestine,* for I dearly desired to see the view upon the other side before the day had faded. But it was night when I reached the summit; the moon was riding high and clear; and only a few gray streaks of twilight lingered in the west. A yawning valley gulfed in blackness, lay like a hole in created nature at my feet; but the outline of the hills was sharp against the sky. There was *Mount Aigoal,* the stronghold of *Castanet.* And *Castanet,* not only as an active undertaking leader, deserves some mention among Camisards; for there is a spray of rose among his laurel; and he showed how, even in a public tragedy, love will have its way. In the high tide of war he married, in his mountain citadel, a young and pretty lass called *Mariette*. There were great rejoicings; and the bridegroom released five-and-twenty prisoners in honor of the glad event. Seven months afterwards *Mariette,* the *Princess of the Cévennes,* as they called her in derision, fell into the hands of the authorities, where it was like to have gone hard with her. But *Castanet* was a man of execution, and loved his wife. He fell on *Valleraugue,* and got a lady there for a hostage; and for the first and last time in that war there was an exchange of prisoners. Their daughter, pledge of some starry night upon *Mount Aigoal,* has left descendants to this day.

Modestine and I—it was our last meal together—had a snack upon the top of *St. Pierre,* I on a heap of stones, she standing by me in the moonlight and decorously eating bread out of my hand. The poor brute would eat more heartily in this manner; for she had a sort of affection for me, which I was soon to betray.

It was a long descent upon *St. Jean du Gard,* and we met no one but a carter, visible afar off by the glint of the moon on his extinguished lantern.

Before ten o'clock we had got in and were at supper; fifteen miles and a stiff hill in little beyond six hours!

FAREWELL, MODESTINE!

ON examination, on the morning of *October 3d*, *Modestine* was pronounced unfit for travel. She would need at least two days' repose according to the ostler; but I was now eager to reach *Alais* for my letters; and, being in a civilized country of stage-coaches, I determined to sell my lady-friend and be off by the diligence that afternoon. Our yesterday's march, with the testimony of the driver who had pursued us up the long hill of *St. Pierre,* spread a favorable notion of my donkey's capabilities. Intending purchasers purchasers were aware of an unrivalled opportunity. Before ten I had an offer of twenty-five francs; and before noon, after a desperate engagement, I sold her, saddle and all, for five-and-thirty. The pecuniary gain is not obvious, but I had bought freedom into the bargain.

St. Jean du Gard is a large place and largely Protestant. The *maire,* a Protestant, asked me to help him in a small matter which is itself characteristic of the country. The young women of the *Cévennes* profit by the common religion and the difference of the language to go largely as governesses into *England;* and here was one, a native of *Mialet,* struggling with English circulars from two different agencies in *London.* I gave what help I could; and volunteered some advice, which struck me as being excellent.

One thing more I note. The *phylloxera* has ravaged the vineyards in this neighborhood; and in the early morning, under some chestnuts by the river, I found a party of men working with a cider-press. I could not at first make out what they were after, and asked one fellow to explain.

"Making cider," he said. *"Oui, c'est comme ça. Comme dans le nord!"*

There was a ring of sarcasm in his voice: the country was going to the devil.

It was not until I was fairly seated by the driver, and rattling through a rocky valley with dwarf olives, that I became aware of my bereavement. I had lost *Modestine*. Up to that moment I had thought I hated her; but now she was gone.

> "And, O,
> The difference to me!"

For twelve days we had been fast companions; we had travelled upwards of a hundred and twenty miles, crossed several respectable ridges, and jogged along with our six legs by many a rocky and many a boggy by-road. After the first day, although sometimes I was hurt and distant in manner, I still kept my patience; and as for her, poor soul! she had come to regard me as a god. She loved to eat out of my hand. She was patient, elegant in form, the color of an ideal mouse, and inimitably small. Her faults were those of her race and sex; her virtues were her own. Farewell, and if forever——

Father Adam wept when he sold her to me; after I had sold her in my turn, I was tempted to follow his example; and being alone with the stage-driver and four or five agreeable young men, I did not hesitate to yield to my emotion.

THE END

AN OBJECT OF PITY

AN OBJECT OF PITY

"LATE, EVER LATE"

THAT was a strange house, fit for a strange inhabitant. The ground on which it stood was low. A tremor and a great voice of the sea filled it day and night. Mouldering gardens, from which the luxuriance of a tropic flora had now almost effaced the artifice of man, came close to its walls, and were studded with lone pavilions, and browsed by costly steeds. Lights passed amid the thickets; lights turn red faintly in the pavilions; in the upper story shone the lamps and lantern of the high festival; in all the lower chambers, tapers of vigilant myrmidons streamed between substantial gratings. For the place was barred with steel, like the heart of him who dwelt there.

Ay, it was a fit free home for him: semi-royal, sinister, senescent; strong enough, in a military point of view, to bear the onset of besieging battalions, and yet tottering to its fall. Bees nested in the beams. By night strange tropic things poured forth, and obscured the bright lamps, and blotted the rare napery, so that, at times, even the Man Haggard would leap in a horror from his festival, and roar until the caverned peninsula trembled and re-echoed to its bowels, and the pale guests and the obsequious alien servants crowded to appease his fury. Costly works of art and deadly instruments of war hung together from the walls; costly and humble gewgaws lay heaped in barbaric incongruity upon the tables; and at times, while the Man Haggard strode in his long unsteady halls, and berated his accomplices, and gave to those weighty

243

dispatches, over which ministers grew pale, the thunder of his voice, then would burn at his side, as it burned in the boudoir of the dissolute hetaira, as in the retiring room of the luxurious Hussar, that rare, that almost priceless perfume, *Ruban de Bruges*. Ay, they were well met, the strange house and its singular denizen, they were well met.

The guests were assembled, the Queen-woman—she who was nameless, but who throned it there like any Berenice or Semiramis of the old glad days, when the world's eyes were young and the kids danced among the capers to the flutes of Pan—the Queen-woman sat in her chair, calm of face, but trouble ate into her heart. For there was one wanting. The dark witch of the mountains stole with small steps, peered with swift uneasy eyes, but peered in vain. Still there was one wanting. In vain Prince Rupert obliterated all expression from his face and veiled an anxious glance behind a shining eye-glass; in vain he gathered admiration from all women, and envy from all men; he, too, felt the omen, and quailed in his gold lace, and he of the name which brought a light to the eye of the Canadian book agent, and a flush to the cheek of the Chicago pirate—he who had earned fame only to despise it, luxury only to discard it—who had fled from the splendours of a suburban residence to toss in the rude trading schooner among uncharted reefs—who had left the saturnalian pleasures of the Athenæum to become a dweller in the bush, and the councillor of rebel sovereigns, crouching at night with them about the draughty lamp on the bare cabin floor—whose pen was of gold, and his bed a mat on a chest, who loved but three things, women, adventure, art—and art the least of these three, and, as men whispered, adventure the most—was he, even he, at ease? I trow not. His slender fingers plucked at his long mustache; his dark eyes glittered in his narrow sanguine face; in his mind—the mind of a poet—the oaths of stevedores and coalporters hurtled.

But these were of those who knew; and meanwhile the ruck of the invited thronged with precaution on the tottering floors. The house was doomed; report ran openly in the island capital that it must fall; perhaps nothing but the fame of the Queen-woman could have gathered so great a company under its menacing roof. And as the wind beat upon its walls and deluged it with volleys of stage-rain, and the beams throbbed under that multitudinous footing, one looked to another with a haggard surmise, and the speech on their pale, silent faces syllabled a common fear: *"Will it fall to-night?"* Outside, in the narrow harbour, under the darkness of the night and storm, huge warships tossed with their ponderous armament; yet these were safe, and that throng of many races, treading the long halls of the Man Haggard, knew themselves in danger. In vain the lamps shone many coloured; in vain the banners drooped and the palms arched on the gorgeous walls. Heart spoke to heart, and their speech was of fear. One thought was in the mind of white and brown; of the hardy American; of the lissom Hindu; of the Teuton, bearded and bald; of the islander, barefoot even in that gay place, and robed in white like a sun-priest of the old, glad days, when the world's eyes were young, and the gods, etc.; of the gilt and glazed Hussar, inured to the thunder of the squadrons; of the captain of the great ships, deafened with the bellowing of the guns; for all these were crowded in the halls of the Man Haggard, and all walked with bated breath.

Ay, they feared that! the innocent, the uncunning; that material fear spoke loud to all; the most ignorant espied, under the flowers and palms, the blackness of the pit. The tale is old; old as the days when the rude Macedonian peasant, bursting his way across Thessalian thickets, saw, and knew, and thrilled at the sight of old Evoe and Dyonisius of Helikarnassos dancing, their godheads laid aside by the triumphal amphoræ on the white fields of thyme, and under the flowering boughs of Lachrimachristi. So was it with the guests of Bel-shazzar and the minions of Sardanapalus. The material peril —ay, they could see that; but it was only the few that spied the darker omen and could read the minatory script upon the wall. There was the strength, the wisdom, the youth, wealth and beauty of the islands, crowded in the halls of the Man Haggard, swinging as they were with the assault of tempest; thronged as were their cellars with treacherous, alien slaves; and the Man Haggard was not there among his guests.

Where was he?

In the extreme rear of his domain, far from the coloured lamps and the stringed music, the man had his dwelling in a cabin of painted wood. A stranger (had he dared) might have wandered for days in that rich, decaying pleasance, and perhaps not remarked the Dwelling of the Master. But the way to its door was known by the costly steed that loved to follow and fondle him, and the wild dove that knew and waited for his coming. It was known by the cringing messengers that stole there all day long, the bearers of letters. For it was here that he received, here that he answered them, without a book, without a Peerage, trusting in the resources of his brain. And when the ready pen had done its work he would call for wine, and laugh aloud with that laugh of his that was noisy as a boy's and cruel as a woman's. Outside and in, the cabin was to match. A female thing, a maid, a nymph of Dian, might fitly have bestowed her narrow limbs in that plain sleeping place. A vessel (rude as a consul's) served him for the toilet. Save for the manly shaving stick, and a chest that contained a few memorials of more innocent years, the singular chamber might be best described as empty. And it was in such surroundings that he fitted to his powerful shoulders a coat that was heavy with gold, and was the gift of an Empress. Ay, an Empress gave it him; but did she know all?

He stood a moment in the almost royal pomp of his attire.

"It was otherwise in Norfolk, happy Norfolk, Land of Story," he sighed.

But the weakness in that stern soul endured but for the instant. He turned, he passed forth into the night and tempest, and bowing his lion crest against the onset of the squalls, moved toward the lights and the music.

"Late—ever late," he murmured.

Scarce a moment more, and in the eyes of his surprised and fascinated guests, the Man Haggard stood and glittered on the threshold, a hollow smile on his face, a scornful excuse upon his tongue.

"At last," breathed the Queen-woman.

And the ruddy face of Tusitala paled with the exquisite relief.